THE AMAZING ADVENTURES OF NATE BANKS

FREEZER BURNED

by
JAKE BELL

cover and comic art by
CHRIS GIARRUSSO

SCHOLASTIC INC.

New York   Toronto   London   Auckland

Sydney   Mexico City   New Delhi   Hong Kong

ISBN 978-0-545-15670-7

Text copyright © 2010 by Jake Bell
Illustrations copyright © 2010 by Scholastic Inc.
All rights reserved. Published by Scholastic Inc.
SCHOLASTIC, APPLE PAPERBACKS, and associated logos
are trademarks and/or registered trademarks of Scholastic Inc.

12 11 10 9 8 7 6 5 4 3 2 1   10 11 12 13 14 15/0

Printed in the U.S.A.   40
First printing, May 2010

To Robert and Chris, for feeding my love of comics and my love of writing.

Contents

I Never Thought I'd Miss Dr. Malcontent

Mrs. Sutcliffe's lectures were worst on Monday afternoons. As I fought to stay awake in fourth period, I couldn't help but think about—and dread—the next four days of listening to our replacement science teacher. Despite my best efforts to look alert, my head lolled forward, then snapped back up with a jolt just as Mrs. Sutcliffe wrapped up her lesson.

"So that's why we put salt into the water when we make spaghetti," Mrs. Sutcliffe concluded.

The class stared blankly at her.

"So to review, when you mix two substances, it creates a what?"

She got no answer.

"A solution," she answered herself. "And the boiling or freezing point of that solution—salt water in our example—will be what? The same as or different from that of the solvent—plain water in this case? It will be different. That's why in colder climates, cities will spread salt on roads to prevent them from icing over. Why? Because the freezing point is what? *Lower*."

You had to feel bad for Mrs. Sutcliffe, the chubby blond home ec teacher who'd been roped into teaching science for the remainder of the year. Not only did she not know the subject—which meant she read every lesson directly from the textbook and was unable to answer any questions—but she was also taking over for the man who'd been the most popular teacher in the school.

"I don't care if he did nearly kill us all," my best friend, Teddy, groaned quietly to me. "Please let us have Dr. Content back."

It had been three weeks since our science teacher, Dr. Content, had donned nuclear-powered armor, renamed himself Dr. Malcontent, and destroyed Ditko Middle School in a battle with Ultraviolet, Kanigher Falls' own superhero.

Ultraviolet could fly and she had superstrength. It was hard to judge how invulnerable she was, but I personally had seen her get blasted through a cinder block wall and hit by a dump truck without receiving so much as a scratch.

She'd also written some of the hardest pop quizzes I'd ever taken.

Ultraviolet just happened to be my sixth-grade history teacher, Ms. Matthews. Of course, only a few people knew that, including me, my obnoxious sister Denise, and my best friends Teddy and Fiona. I liked to think of myself as a sort of superhero advisor. Regardless of how I thought of myself, though, Ultraviolet thought of me as a twelve-year-old kid who shouldn't be mixed up in her life, especially after I almost died helping her fight Dr. Malcontent.

It's not as bad as it sounds. I got a couple of scrapes and bruises, but considering that I plummeted almost eleven miles from the stratosphere to the school's football field, things really could have been much worse. But until Ultraviolet recognized the value of my advice, I was stuck just doing my math homework after school instead of helping her fight crime. For the record, I'd like to point out that I was the one who figured out how to defeat Dr. Malcontent! Without me, where would she be?

Well, at the moment, she, like the rest of us, was stuck

at Eisner Middle School, where the superintendent had decided to have all the Ditko kids bussed every day until our school could be rebuilt. Fortunately, we'd just gotten good news on that front.

"Three minutes," Teddy sighed, looking at the clock. "Three minutes and we're out of here."

The city had been weighing bids from several companies to rebuild our school until Colleen Collins Construction stepped in with an offer the city couldn't refuse. In addition to donating four million dollars toward the construction effort, Colleen Collins had also purchased several shuttered old factories in the industrial zones near the city reservoir. I wasn't sure why that mattered, but my dad thought it did. He used accountant terms like "property taxes" and "revenue" to try to explain how it would help the city, but I didn't understand any of it.

Colleen Collins was rich and famous, though it seemed the only thing she was famous for was being rich. Whenever there was a big movie premiere, Colleen Collins was there. When someone was throwing the biggest party of the year, Colleen Collins wound up on the guest list. In addition to basically paying to rebuild our school, Colleen Collins had offered to help the city raise more money by displaying her family's pride and joy, the Princess diamond—the third-largest diamond in the world—at the Kanigher Falls Historical Society Museum for a special three-month exhibition.

All I cared about was that the Ditko kids were leaving during fifth period to take buses to the empty lot where our school used to be to attend a ground-breaking ceremony. The Eisner students weren't too happy with the news. There had always been tension between the two student bodies, but it had been escalated by the inconvenience of our situation. No one appreciated the crowded classrooms, longer lunch lines, and tightly packed hallways. And finding out that we were leaving school early on a Monday to see a celebrity rubbed several of the Eisner kids the wrong way.

"Must be nice to get to do whatever you want," one Eisner student said to his friends in the hall between classes, making sure he was loud enough for any Ditko kids to hear him.

"Give them a break. The superintendent probably figures they're too stupid to learn anything in class, so why bother? Might as well send them home early," joked another.

Eisner students tossed insults at Ditko students, who tossed back more at Eisner kids. No one was left out and everyone was a target. Well, except one person. Me.

"Nate! Hey, slow down," called Zach Jeter, an Eisner kid who had desperately been trying to make friends with me since my first day there. He caught up and slapped me across the back. "How's it going? I heard you guys are getting out early. Lucky!"

"I guess so," I replied, walking a bit faster.

"How was your weekend? Did you get to hang out with Ultraviolet? When are we going to do something?" he persisted, matching my pace.

"I didn't get to hang out with Ultraviolet," I assured him. "I see her every day, but I wouldn't call what we do hanging out. I'm her advisor." Okay, maybe that wasn't exactly the truth, but the only reason Zach was even speaking to me was that he'd seen me on TV with Ultraviolet, so I didn't feel the need to be completely honest with him.

"Right," Zach said. "Cool, man. Well, next time you see her, tell her I said hi. And maybe you could get me an autograph."

I shrugged, not at all in the mood to explain to yet

another person that Ultraviolet didn't sign autographs. Ever since I'd been on the news with her for about seven seconds, everyone I knew—and several people I didn't know—had asked me to get autographs or to set up meetings with her.

"Sorry, Zach, but this is my history class," I said with a smile, pointing at the door to Ms. Matthews's temporary room. I was relieved that I could get away from the kid. "I guess I'll see you tomorrow."

Groundbreaking

The way some kids were bounding onto the buses, you'd have thought it was a Friday or the last day of school even though it was just a regular old Monday in late October.

"What's the big deal with Colleen Collins, anyway?" Teddy grumbled as he shoved what looked like a small black pressboard coffin into the seat across from me and sat down. Unlike the rest of the crowd, Teddy was less than thrilled about the groundbreaking ceremony, because it meant he had to play his tuba with the school marching band.

"Well, her grandfather made millions by opening a chain of motels during the Eisenhower administration, when the American highways were being built from coast to coast," Fiona piped up. Teddy's simple question prompted a mini history lesson from Fiona on the life and times of Colleen Collins. She spent the entire bus ride explaining how the debutante's grandfather invested his millions and turned them into billions, creating an existence for his granddaughter that assured she would never have to work a day in her life. Colleen Collins dubbed herself the "American princess," claiming her beauty and upbringing made her the closest thing to royalty the country had. She became a mainstay of the newspaper gossip columns and a regular topic on TV entertainment shows.

"Her entire life is dedicated to being seen surrounded by other celebrities, decked out in pink outfits with her Chihuahua tucked into her handbag," Fiona moaned.

"Yeah, I get it," I said with a sigh. "So why is she digging dirt at a construction site in Kanigher Falls?"

"She's slipping in popularity," Fiona said. "She made that pop album that tanked, her movie closed the same weekend it opened, and that TV show made her look terrible."

"I don't know if she really deserves the blame for *Slashing through the Snow*," I said. "It was a Christmas-themed horror movie, but they released it in April. Besides, the only part anyone said was good was the part with her in it."

"That's because she couldn't read a cereal box, much less a Hollywood script," Fiona countered. "The only reason people liked the scene where she was thrown into a wood chipper along with the discarded Christmas trees was that it meant they didn't have to watch or listen to her anymore."

Even worse than the album and the movie was her self-produced reality show, which became most famous for the episode in which she used her family's influence to meet with about a dozen senators and congressmen to convince them to pass a law naming unicorns an endangered species. "I've never even seen one in real life," she told them in a clip that had been one of the most watched on YouTube for months. All the senators had to agree they hadn't ever seen a real unicorn, either.

"Worst of all, *Celebs* magazine's Hot 'n' Not list declared her 'Not' in three of the last four months," Fiona noted. I almost pointed out that her knowing this meant she had to have been reading *Celebs* magazine regularly for the last four months, but somehow I managed to stop myself.

"She needs a public relations boost and thinks donating money to build a new school will help change her image," Fiona concluded.

I suspected there was more to it than that. After winning the bid, Colleen had suggested a big ground-breaking ceremony and had invited Ultraviolet to shovel the first clump of dirt with a golden shovel. Unfortunately, Ultraviolet had declined the invitation.

If I could get Ms. Matthews to talk about it, I'm sure she would say it was because she had to attend the ceremony as a teacher, and she and Ultraviolet can't be in the same place at the same time. Personally, I figured she just didn't like the public aspect of being a superhero. Waving to crowds, cutting ribbons at grand openings, signing autographs—none of those things appealed to her. Ultraviolet preferred to fly in, save the day, and get back to class in time to finish a lecture about Roosevelt's New Deal.

As we got off the bus, Teddy shuffled over to the area where the marching band was gathering.

"Is she here yet?" I asked Fiona as we jostled for a spot in the crowd.

Fiona gestured over her shoulder to where a stretch limousine was parked. A man in a black chauffeur's outfit stood at attention beside it. Photographers snapped pictures, waiting for the door to open. "I don't know," Fiona said dryly. "She might be around here somewhere."

I glanced at the band and caught sight of Teddy. The band wasn't much of a marching band. They were barely a *playing* band. Teddy smiled and waved from behind his tuba. I returned the wave and the crowd gasped and swooned. For a moment I was shocked so many people would be so affected by my simple gesture, but then I realized that the limo's doors had opened.

The school band struck up a poor rendition of "Louie Louie," because it was the only song they knew. Colleen, flanked by a pair of bodyguards and a frazzled woman who seemed to be her personal assistant, strode to the ceremonial square of dirt on legs too skinny to support the weight of a healthy woman her age. Her eyes were hidden behind large designer sunglasses that perched atop a nose that appeared to be the attempt of one of Beverly Hills' finest plastic surgeons to re-create the nose of a prettier girl. Her smile resembled that of a dog with peanut butter stuck to the roof of its mouth.

"And she makes her living as a model," Fiona muttered, shaking her head.

"She makes her living asking her dad for money," I laughed.

The superintendent of the school district and Principal Gwynn greeted Colleen at the square of dirt. A pink ribbon that matched her outfit was tied around the handle of the shovel. The three shook hands and exchanged greetings for a moment before Colleen's personal assistant began barking orders to some of the photographers, and moving the superintendent and principal around as if they were chess pieces.

"What's that all about?" I asked.

"Her job is to make sure they get perfect pictures for tomorrow's papers," Mr. Dawson, who'd overheard us, answered. "The publicist has to make sure everyone sees Colleen looking just right. It takes a lot of time and coordination to make something look spontaneous and unplanned."

The band continued to play the same sixteen bars of "Louie Louie" it had been playing continually for almost six minutes. Teddy's face was red and his eyes were watering as he kept belting out a repeated series of ten notes over and over. BUM BUM BUM . . . BA BA BA BA BA . . . BUM BUM!

At long last, Principal Gwynn stepped forward, waving his arms to the crowd. He welcomed everyone to the site of the new Ditko Middle School and extended special thanks to both Superintendent Lee and Colleen Collins. The band finally stopped playing, and Teddy slumped in his chair, gasping for breath and pinching his lips to regain feeling in them.

"We have been so fortunate in light of the tragedy that befell our old school," our principal recited. "So many of us watched as our school, our home away from home, was torn to pieces by forces beyond our comprehension. We watched from — many of us from right over there." He pointed to a spot across the street where several evacuated classes had gathered while Ultraviolet and Dr. Malcontent had battled each other. "When I saw the rubble, when I saw the devastation, I feared this day might never come. But because of our strong community and because of the generosity of Miss Collins, I am so very excited not only to have Ditko Middle School back, but to know this new school will be better than we could ever have imagined! So, without any further ado, I present our special guest"—he glanced down at an index card and read word for word—"the American princess, Colleen Collins."

A sprinkling of applause made its way through the crowd. The principal gestured to Colleen. It took her a moment to realize that the sweeping of his arms toward the crowd was an invitation for her to talk. "Yeah, well . . ." She paused and seemed to be searching for some inspirational words for the occasion. "It's just nice to be able to help out and stuff? Because, y'know, like, Kanigher Falls is a cool place? And I kind of was all, um, 'Hey, is Ultraviolet going to be there?' But I guess she's just busy saving the world or something?"

I stole a glance at Ms. Matthews, who stood near the back of the crowd.

"So I guess, like, this town is pretty cool and stuff?" Colleen continued, raising her voice at the end of every sentence, which made it sound like she was asking a series of questions. "I bought a bunch of those factories and we're going to bulldoze them? Oh, and go see the Princess diamond, okay? So where's the shovel?"

The superintendent stepped up with the shovel and

handed it to Colleen. The band belted out another unending loop of "Louie Louie" while she took a lame stab at the square of dirt, dropped the shovel, and retreated toward her limo, waving and smiling at the photographers the entire time.

One of Colleen's bodyguards, who resembled a shaved gorilla, cleared a path through the crowd. He pushed people out of the way as he headed straight toward us. Another bodyguard—this one smaller and wiry, with spiked hair and a goatee—reached out to push me away.

"Make a path here, people," he barked. "We need to get Miss Collins to an important appointment." He put his hand on my shoulder, and my entire arm went numb. He must have used some kind of secret ninja nerve pinch on me. I stood there, no doubt with a stupid look on my face, trying to regain the feeling in my arm as Colleen Collins passed by, just feet away.

Suddenly, she stopped. "Hey, you're that guy who was on the news with Ultraviolet?" she recalled. She pointed a finger at me.

"That's him," Fiona chimed in. "Nate Banks, superhero sidekick."

"I'm not really a sidekick," I assured both of them. "I was really just a hostage."

"Cool!" gushed Colleen. "Do you ever see Ultraviolet anymore?"

"I—I've, um . . . well, a couple of times, yeah," I stammered, not wanting to say too much.

"Well, the next time you see her, tell her I really want to meet her? She's just great and stuff? I'm going to be in Kanigher Falls a lot now, because I'm building this school? And I just bought some old factories on the north side of town, but we're going to tear those down and build—oh, you know what?" She wheeled around and grabbed her personal assistant by the collar. "Take this down!" she barked.

The assistant opened a leather notebook and got a pen ready.

"Nate Banks, right?" Colleen asked with a friendly giggle. The assistant started scratching in the notebook. "Tomorrow afternoon we'll be unveiling the Princess diamond at the museum? How about you come, and bring your whole class? You can be the very first people in Kanigher Falls to see it?"

I didn't care much about seeing a diamond, but going would mean another day off, so I didn't dare turn it down. "Sure!" I agreed enthusiastically. "I should probably ask one of my teach—"

Ms. Matthews had made her way over to where we were talking. She eyed me suspiciously.

"There she is. Ms. Matthews, Colleen Collins wants our class to go see the Princess diamond tomorrow. Can we go?"

I knew she wouldn't say no. After all, she was a history teacher, and the diamond would be displayed at the Historical Society.

"And tell Ultraviolet to call me if she wants to come, too?" Colleen Collins said as she grabbed me weakly by the shoulders, leaned forward, and kissed the air next to both my cheeks. I laughed politely as she made her way to the limousine.

"Wow, you know Colleen Collins?" a voice behind me said excitedly.

It was Allison Heaton. Normally, a seventh-grade girl would never talk to a sixth-grade boy, but I guess this was a special exception. Before I could answer, Teddy, who'd managed to get out from behind his tuba to join us, pushed me aside.

"Hey, Allison," Teddy said, dropping his voice an octave or two. Back when we were in first grade,

Teddy first set eyes on the tall, blond second grader Allison and fell in love on the spot. Unfortunately, in the ensuing five years, she hadn't noticed him.

She turned and smiled politely. "Hi, Neddy." Allison never got Teddy's name right, though he preferred to focus on the silver lining that she always got his name wrong the same way. He believed that her thinking his name was Ned instead of Ted proved that she knew who he was.

"Nate, I'm having a Halloween party at my house this Saturday," Allison said sweetly. "Would you like to come?"

Teddy's fingers dug into my arm. "Sure," I said through a pained wince. "Sounds like fun."

"Yes!" Teddy whispered.

Allison smiled and went back to her friends. Fiona rolled her eyes at Teddy and made a fake gagging sound.

That's Why I Punched Him in the Stomach

Riding home from school after the groundbreaking with Teddy and his tuba was even more difficult than it sounds. It wasn't like he could heft the thing onto the back of a bicycle, so he had no choice but to walk, lugging the tuba case. He had to stop every ten yards or so to rest his arms and reestablish his grip on the handles. Meanwhile, Fiona and I rode our bikes as slowly as we could, but even that wasn't slow enough. To avoid tumbling over sideways, we had to continually double back, circling around Teddy and his tuba case like two vultures waiting for him to drop.

"What was the point of that ridiculous ceremony?" Fiona asked as she rode away from me and looped around.

"Don't complain," Teddy replied. "We got out of class for an hour, even if it was for something stupid."

"That just means we have more homework to make up for the classes we missed," Fiona pointed out. "And why? So we could go see some brainless woman smile for the cameras?"

"Hey!" I protested. "Miss Collins is helping to pay for our new school. Plus she seemed pretty nice."

Fiona stared at me like I had a fish growing out of my forehead. "A few compliments and a chance to get out of school for a field trip? Is that seriously all it takes to win you over?"

"It's good enough for me," Teddy insisted. "Especially if it gets us into Allison Heaton's Halloween party this weekend."

"I didn't hear Allison invite you," Fiona pointed out. "I heard her say"—she switched to a high-pitched, vapid voice—"'*Whoa, Nate, you're so awesome because you know some celebrities even though you don't really know them. You should totally come to my party. Oh, and don't bring Neddy, because if I liked him at all, I probably would have learned his real name sometime in the last five years.*'"

Teddy seemed to deflate as this truth sank in. "Yeah,"

he reluctantly agreed, "I suppose you're right." With a defeated grunt, he hefted the tuba case and trudged forward.

A block later, Fiona said good-bye and rode down her street to her house. Suddenly, I felt silly circling my best friend. I hopped off my bike to walk beside him.

"Teddy, I promise I'll talk to Allison," I said. "I'll get you an invitation. And if I can't, then I won't go. I don't want to go to some stupid party if my best friend can't be there, too."

He looked back at me as he set down the case to rest his arms. "Thanks," he replied meekly. "But you don't have to do that for me. I want you to go."

"No, I'm serious," I assured him. "I really don't want to go unless you can come, too. It sounds completely boring."

Teddy lifted his tuba case to continue our walk. "You don't have to say that just to make me feel bett—"

A second later, I was in a bush, struggling to escape a tangle of branches and my bicycle, which had fallen on top of me. Teddy was on the ground, pinned beneath his instrument. Meathead McCaskill was perched on top of the tuba case, staring down menacingly at the helpless Teddy.

Meathead McCaskill was the biggest bully in town. He had long made a living by strong-arming kids for their lunch money. He was the reason I had eaten sandwiches out of brown paper bags every day for the last three years. Originally, I'd had a lunch box, but to Meathead a lunch box is just something to smash over a victim's head while you berate him for not bringing money to buy himself lunch.

Because he'd failed three grades, he was older and bigger than anyone else at the school. Thick black hair covered his massive forearms, which looked like two hams sticking out of the ends of his sleeves. By this point in the afternoon, he had a shadow of whiskers sprouting on his chin and cheeks. I tried to ignore all this as I emerged from the thicket, covered in scratches and leaves.

"Gimme your money!" Meathead threatened, cocking his fist.

Pinned beneath the massive black case and a kid twice his size, Teddy couldn't have moved to get his money even if he'd had any. Of course, neither of us brought money to school for exactly this reason.

I balled up my fists as I lunged from the bush. Unfortunately, the rustling of leaves and the clattering of my bike alerted Meathead that I was back on my feet, and he spun to greet me, his fist drawn back to strike. "Oh, hey, Banks," he said with a smile, dropping his fist. "How's it goin'?"

My fists tightened, but my arms hung limply at my sides, unsure what to make of this reaction. "It—it was going okay, I suppose," I stammered. "Until you shoved me into that bush."

"Sorry about that," he apologized sheepishly. "I didn't notice it was you."

I heard Teddy groan softly.

"Oh, Banks, check this out." Meathead turned his attention back to Teddy. "Give me your money, Cochrane," he threatened with a growl. "Or I'm gonna squeeze you like a *tuba* toothpaste." He looked back at me with a smile. "Get it? Tuba?" He slapped the case to drive home the point, and Teddy yelped in pain.

"Oh, right," I agreed. "Good one."

"I thought of it when I noticed he had a tuba." Meathead beamed, tapping his temple with his finger.

"Clever," I chuckled nervously. I looked over and saw that Teddy had gotten out from under the case and was struggling to his feet. "So, we don't have any money—"

"Don't worry about it, Banks," Meathead said with a wave of his hand. "If I'd realized it was you, I never would have tossed you into that bush." I winced as his big meaty hand swung toward me, but he merely brushed some leaves gently from my shoulder. "Sorry about that."

I tried to keep a smile on my face while I made my way over to Teddy and helped him up. When I turned back, Meathead was untwisting a branch from my bike wheel's spokes.

"Hey, Banks," he said as he put down the kickstand. "The next time Ultraviolet comes to see you, do you think you could kinda get me . . . maybe an autograph or something?"

I breathed in deeply, not sure what to tell him. "Uh, well, see, the thing is, Ultraviolet doesn't really come to see me."

Meathead screwed up his face in anger but quickly relaxed it as if suddenly getting a joke. "Right. She doesn't come around to see you. Like she didn't come rescue you at the old school and she didn't come be on the news with you at the new school. I get it." He leaned toward me and spoke in a low, conspiratorial tone. "Well, the next time she *doesn't come around,* can you get me an autograph?"

"I'll see what I can do," I agreed.

"Great!" He turned to Teddy. "Now, Cochrane. Gimme your money."

Teddy stood upright in disbelief. "Nate told you I don't have any mon—"

Meathead buried his fist in Teddy's stomach. My best friend found himself back on the ground, gasping for air.

"Whoa!" I shouted, leaning down to help Teddy back to his feet. "What was that for? You said you didn't mean to attack us."

"I said I didn't mean to throw *you* into the bush."

"Well, Teddy's my best friend."

"And I respect that," Meathead replied solemnly. "That's why I only punched him in the stomach. Probably won't even leave a bruise."

Teddy looked up at me, his eyes red. "Being your friend sure has its benefits."

We're Here to Learn, People!

As our bus pulled up in front of the Kanigher Falls Historical Society Museum, I looked up to see police snipers lining the roofs of the surrounding office buildings. My friends and I got off the bus and saw a team of seven police motorcycles rolling slowly down the empty street in a V formation, like a flock of geese heading south. Behind them were two armored cars and six police cruisers. Every car and motorcycle had its red and blue lights flashing.

Once we stepped inside the museum, a curator greeted us. She explained that more than half the Kanigher Falls Police Department and a few officers on loan from the Everett PD were assigned to ensure the secure transportation of the gem to the Kanigher Falls Historical Society Museum.

The curator led us into a climate-controlled room that held nothing but an empty glass case, where the diamond would be installed.

"Inside each of those armored cars you saw outside is a safe," the curator explained. "Neither can be opened without a seven-digit code and two keys. Both the codes and the keys are en route from different locations in nondescript cars and are held by people who have never met. Inside each safe is a metal briefcase with two combination locks. If the wrong combination is entered into the lock, a mechanism in the case fills the room with sleeping gas. Inside each briefcase is a titanium box with a blue liquid-crystal pad for scanning thumbprints. Only members of the Collins family can open those boxes."

And inside only one of the titanium boxes, she continued, was the third-largest diamond in the world, the famed Princess diamond.

Once the curator finished describing all the security to us, a guide arrived to take us on a tour of the museum's historical exhibits until the diamond was secured and ready for installation.

"When prospectors found deposits of gold in the waters at the base of Kanigher Falls in August of

1871, word spread quickly," the museum guide said as he gestured toward a large display about gold mining. "By October, the town's population had grown to more than twelve times what it had been. In less than a year, Kanigher Falls had become the third-largest town in the Southwest."

This was the third time in my life I'd been to the Kanigher Falls Historical Society Museum and the second time I'd heard this lecture. Prospectors came for gold. When the gold ran out, they left, but the buildings and roads and businesses and rails remained, and the town got a boost from the condiment industry. Pickles, mustard, ketchup, and sauerkraut—just about anything you could put on a hot dog or a hamburger—had been manufactured in a block of factories on the north side of town. At least until they were lured away by cheaper labor. It's not the most amazing story.

Most of the items in the glass cases throughout the museum were things like bonnets that settler women had worn, wheels from covered wagons, tools used by prospectors, and railroad lanterns. It had all been on display there for decades before any of us were born, so nobody got too excited.

Since I knew most of the material being covered, I used much of my time trying to get close enough to Ms. Matthews to talk to her about some of my plans to help her out. She knew I wanted to talk, and she did everything she could to avoid me. She walked away from me, shushed me when I started to speak, even sent me out to the bus to get jackets for some of the kids who'd left them but were cold.

"To our left, you'll see what might appear to be two ordinary rocks," the guide was saying as I returned from the bus with the jackets. "However, these were used in the 1800s to grind corn."

I handed the jackets to Ms. Matthews. "Here are the—"

"Nate Banks?" a familiar voice called out.

Colleen Collins pushed her way through my classmates to get to me. Well, technically, her bodyguard did most of the pushing, and she simply followed in his wake. With each person they passed, more eyes followed them, until Colleen stopped in front of me.

"Oh, it *is* you!" She threw her arms out like she was going to hug me, but instead put her fingertips softly on my shoulders, leaned forward, and kissed the air beside both my cheeks in the "American princess" greeting. "What a coincidence! Why are you here?"

The other students were whispering among themselves. "Um, you invited us."

"Oh, right!" she said with a giggle. Then she looked around at the rest of the students as if she'd just noticed them. "You mean you're in charge of all these guys?"

"Well, not exactly—"

"Wait until you see the diamond. It looks a-*maz*-ing!" she gushed giddily. "It's too pretty to be here with all this boring old stuff. I mean, why is there so much old stuff here, anyway?"

"Well . . . it is a history museum," I said.

"I know, right?" she replied. "I talked to the cura—cruelter?—you know, the head lady? And I'm like, 'Here's some money I want to donate!' So now maybe they can buy some new history? So it's not all so old?"

"New hist—" Ms. Matthews tried to jump in, but was cut off.

"I mean, look at that tomahawk?" Colleen pointed toward one of the cases. "That thing's probably, like, a million years old or something."

"Actually, one hundred fifty," Ms. Matthews corrected, but Colleen ignored her.

"Oh, Nate!" Colleen giggled again. "As long as I have you here, were you able to tell Ultraviolet how much I want to meet her?"

Out of the corner of my eye, I could see Ms. Matthews glaring. "Not exactly," I told Colleen. "I've been trying to, but she's been busy. I was going to tell her this morning, but she had to go rescue somebody. A fire, I think."

Colleen looked a little suspicious.

"I promise you I'll talk to her today," I assured her. I glanced at Ms. Matthews long enough to catch her disapproving frown.

Colleen, on the other hand, was smiling. "Thank you, Nate!" she shrieked. "You're the best!" Another weak hug and pair of air kisses, and she was gone. Unfortunately for me, the stares of my classmates remained.

"Come on," I shouted to the museum guide. "Tell us more about the territorial prison in Russheath. We're here to learn, people!" The guide continued with his speech, pointing to a pair of rusty iron shackles used on the prisoners, but there were more people paying attention to me than to him.

We made it through the rest of the guided tour and were ushered back into the room with the Princess diamond exhibit. After a long wait, Colleen Collins walked in with two of her bodyguards and several well-armed police officers, including one who carried a small metal box.

"Okay, people, it's finally here," Colleen announced. She clapped her hands like a small child. Then she pulled out an index card and started reading aloud. "This diamond has been in my family for, like, a zillion years, ever since my grandpa bought it in 1956. It was first discovered somewhere in Africa in 1897, and it's the largest jewel in the world owned by someone who's not royalty. Except that I might as well be royalty. America doesn't have any royalty, so I'm like an American princess. And speaking of princesses, here is the Princess diamond."

Colleen Collins stepped up, flanked by her body-guards, and pressed her thumb against the pad on the box in the police officer's hands. He opened it, and handed the box to the larger of the bodyguards while the thin one took out the diamond with a gloved hand. He held it up so that Colleen could examine it and the rest of us could see the sheer size of the thing. The Princess was as big as a small child's shoe.

Colleen Collins half looked at it and nodded her approval. The bodyguard gently reached into the case and placed the diamond on a velvet stand. The stand rested on a weight sensor and was surrounded by lasers, infrared heat sensors, motion detectors, and a list of other especially expensive security features Colleen insisted on bragging about. Once the case was sealed, we were allowed to file past, though I didn't get my turn.

Instead, Colleen Collins dragged me away for another discussion.

"It's a shame Ultraviolet couldn't be here today," she began.

"Well, she's a busy, um, superhero."

"Did you tell her I invited her myself?"

"She . . . yes. She got your invitation."

"Nate, I need to know something," Colleen whispered conspiratorially. "You say you're an advisor to her, right?"

"Yes."

"Is that true? Because one of my bodyguards suspects that Ultraviolet—in his words—wouldn't know you from a monkey? He thinks you're trying to fool me?"

"No. Noooo. Not me. I don't know what I can tell you. I mean, I talk to Ultraviolet every day. She's around me all the time. Even now, you may not see her here, but she's here. You know? Trust me. She's watching me like a hawk."

"I believe you, Nate." Colleen smiled. "I'm glad to hear that." She grabbed my shoulders and did her weird kiss thing again. I saw Ms. Matthews watching us from across the room. Colleen went back to her bodyguards and I walked toward my teacher. For the first time all day, she wasn't avoiding me.

"Why don't we talk?" she said.

The World Isn't Spinning, We Are!

While the rest of the students boarded the bus, Ms. Matthews and I stayed back.

"I assume the thing you needed to tell me was that Colleen Collins is just dying to meet me," she said with a hint of annoyance.

"No, you already know that," I said. "I just can't bring myself to tell her you're not going to do it. I've just wanted to talk to you about ways I can help you."

"Help me what?" Ms. Matthews asked impatiently.

"Help you"—I looked around to make sure no one could hear, and lowered my voice so it was just above a whisper—"be Ultraviolet. Like when we fought Dr. Malcontent."

Ms. Matthews shook her head sharply. "No, Nate.

I can't do that. You almost died when I fought Dr. Malcontent."

"But you saved me, so it's all good."

"I wouldn't have had to save you if I hadn't been stupid enough to fly you into the stratosphere and drop you in the first place."

"Considering that was the first time you'd ever fought a supervillain, I think you did a pretty good job," I said reassuringly.

"I can't put you or anyone else in a position like that again, Nate," she said firmly. "I appreciate that you want to help, and yes, your advice was quite helpful in the past, but it's not worth your life."

I tried to argue, but she held up a hand to stop me. She pointed toward the bus, where the rest of the students and teachers were waiting. Frustrated, I hopped aboard only to find all the seats filled. Walking down the aisle, I was nearly hit by Gabe Alomar falling out of his seat.

"Nate," Zach Jeter said warmly, patting the now empty seat beside him, "I saved you a seat."

"That's okay," I insisted. "I can just squeeze in with Teddy and Fiona back there."

Zach gave Gabe a nasty look and mumbled, "Get!"

between his teeth. Then he grabbed my arm and dragged me into the seat. "No need for that when there's room right here, buddy."

The bus pulled away from the museum. Out the window I could see Colleen Collins, flanked by two bodyguards, getting into a limousine parked near the entrance. How long would it be before I'd see her again? Every time I turned around, she was there asking if I'd talked to Ultraviolet. I got the impression that even if I told her she was never going to meet Ultraviolet, that wasn't going to get her off my back.

Once the bus started moving, Zach wouldn't stop talking. "You know, when I first saw you, I said, 'That kid seems pretty cool.' Don't take this the wrong way, but you don't seem like a Ditko kid. You're like us Eisner kids."

Accuse me of not having enough school spirit, but I wasn't in the mood to argue the merits of Eisner Middle School versus Ditko Middle School at the time—even though the irrigation canal behind Eisner makes the entire school smell like horse manure. Instead, I just let Zach ramble on, and I shrugged occasionally to give the impression I was listening. We started across the Moldoff Bridge, which was only about three miles from school, and I breathed a deep sigh of relief that the bus ride was almost over.

"—because kids from Ditko are all like, 'Cheeseburgers are better,' but Eisner kids know hamburgers are the best. I mean, sure you can put cheese on top of a hamburger, but that's still a hamburger."

"What?" I asked. "Did you just say hamburgers with cheese on top are better than cheeseburgers?"

"You know it!" He put up a hand for a high five. "I knew you were an Eisner kid!"

"A cheeseburger *is* a hamburger with cheese on top. That makes no sense."

"Huh?" Zach looked confused.

"That's like saying a turkey sandwich is better than two slices of bread with turkey between them," I argued. "How can you—"

Suddenly, I noticed that the river outside the window was rotating away from the bus. In fact, the entire world was spinning around us. I stood and glanced at the rest of the windows. Ever so slowly, the road moved from the windshield in front of the driver to the side windows, and the river that I'd been looking at over the side of the bridge moved to the emergency exit door in the back. What could possibly be causing the bridge to spin? In an instant, I realized that the world wasn't spinning, we were.

The bus had turned almost entirely backward, and out the windshield we could see cars driving toward us. The drivers all looked panicked. The bus driver wrestled with the steering wheel, but that had no effect. It was as though we were floating just inches off the road with no way to stop. That's not entirely accurate. There was one way to stop.

Perpendicular to the road, the bus hit the steel-and-concrete railing along the edge of the bridge. All of us on the bus were thrown forward into the backs of the seats in front of us. A piece of the railing tore a gash in the side of the bus, narrowly missing the legs of a half dozen students. The windshield and front doors were spiderwebbed with cracks, but the safety glass prevented them from raining shards on us all. Out my window, I could see the Moldoff River about fifty feet below. From what I could tell, the front wheels and about a third of the bus were hanging off the edge of the bridge.

"Okay, don't panic," the bus driver yelled. He stood and staggered. "We're going to have to exit out the back. One at a time! Don't push!"

One of the Eisner teachers made his way to the back and jerked the emergency handle. Things were pretty orderly as everyone pulled themselves together and made for the exit like a sore, confused conga line.

Then the bus shifted.

Because the kids in the back got out first, the back of the bus got lighter. That meant the heavier front started to dip a little more toward the river. Everyone waiting to get out lurched backward an inch or two, but an inch or two was all it took to start a panic. Soon everyone was shoving and trying to climb over the seats to get out.

Metal groaned as the bus slid forward and the aisle became steeper. Waiting in line, I thought for the first time about Ms. Matthews. She was sitting quietly toward the front of the bus. Bracing myself against the seat backs, I clambered down to her.

"What are you doing? We need to get out—" Then I saw what she was doing. With both hands, she was gripping the steel railing that had torn through the side of the bus. By holding the railing and pushing back against the bus with her back and legs, she was preventing us from falling into the river. Or at least, she was delaying our fall.

"It's not going to hold much longer, Nate," she grunted. It wasn't that she wasn't strong enough; the bus wasn't. The seat she was sitting in was buckling, and the steel side of the bus was tearing like paper. It was like trying to lift a grocery bag full of watermelons by the thin plastic handles. No matter how strong you might be, you were going to have a big splattered mess.

Only about a dozen students remained in line. I scrambled up the slope toward them. There were two other emergency exits, on the sides of the bus, but one was hanging over the river and the other was smashed into the concrete railing, which was why the driver had told us—

The driver!

A quick glance at the front of the bus confirmed my fear. He'd never passed me on the way to the back. After telling us to get off, he had collapsed and was lying halfway down the stairs at the entrance. I rushed to help him up, Ms. Matthews shouting at me as I passed her.

Fortunately, the driver wasn't unconscious, just very dazed. With my help, he got to his feet. The last of the students were leaping out the back, so we had a clear path, though it didn't look like it was going to be easy. Every second, the slope got steeper. Both the driver and I had to pull ourselves forward using the seats like rungs on a ladder, but I also had to help support him so he wouldn't go tumbling to the floor each time the bus shifted.

Finally, we reached the back exit and he tried to pull himself out. With my shoulder planted in the small of his back and my legs braced against two of the seats, I pushed him out the door.

And then my foot slipped.

It was impossible to tell what was up and what was down as I rolled down the aisle, bouncing off seats like a pinball. I heard Ms. Matthews shout "Nate!" as I rolled past her, which told me I was close to the front just in time for me to smash back-first into the silver handle that opens the front doors.

"Nate, you have to get out now!" Ms. Matthews shouted over the squeal of bending steel. I looked up at the exit and the trek I had just taken with the bus driver, knowing it would be even harder this time. There was no way for Ms. Matthews to grab me and get us both out in time. With her superspeed, she could probably get herself to the exit once she let go, but if she came toward me, we'd both be trapped in a falling bus. The only way to save us would be to reveal her secret identity by flying out of the wreckage in her work clothes, carrying me in her arms.

As I shifted against the handle that was jabbing me in the back, I accidentally opened the doors. Outside them hung some steel cables that had been knocked loose in the crash.

"Go ahead and let go," I told Ms. Matthews.

She looked unsure.

"Just make sure you come back for me!"

I kicked the door the rest of the way open and leaned out to grab the cables, snaking them around my arms.

Seconds later, I was deafened by the groaning metal of the bus giving up, like a huge yellow-and-black monster's death rattle. In a blur, it shot past me and hit the water below not with a big, pretty, soft splash but with the hard, loud smash you'd expect if it had been dropped on cement. The impact made me grip the cables that much tighter.

"Hold on, Nate," Ms. Matthews yelled. I looked up and saw that she was effortlessly reeling in the cable. Then I heard another voice.

"Step aside, ma'am! I'll get him." Ms. Matthews gently lowered me back down with an apologetic look on her face. She disappeared and was replaced by a man in a dark suit and sunglasses. I recognized him as Colleen Collins's bulkier bodyguard.

Fortunately, he was able to pull me up almost as quickly as Ms. Matthews had, and within seconds I was back on solid ground. Sure enough, Colleen Collins was there. She made her way to my side immediately.

"Are you all right?" she asked. "Oh, Nate, I thought you were dead! I kept waiting for Ultraviolet to show up and save you. Where do you think she might be?"

I shook my head and muttered, "I don't know." The pain in my back and arms was only just starting to register.

"Well, if you see her, be sure to tell her how I saved you," Colleen said sweetly.

"How . . . *you* saved me?" I asked, incredulous.

"No need to thank me. Just doing what I can to make the world a safer place. I guess Ultraviolet and I have a lot in common, huh?"

I nodded to her bigger bodyguard and thanked him.

"No problem," he replied, but Colleen gave him a

sharp look and clamped her fingers shut in a gesture anyone would recognize as meaning "shut up." The guard stepped back, looking embarrassed, and joined the thinner one, who was watching the skies through his blue glasses, no doubt for signs of Ultraviolet's approach.

At last, fire trucks and ambulances showed up. There were some skinned knees and some bumped heads, but most of the students checked out fine. The bus driver was bandaged up and rushed to the hospital, and even though I was just a little sore, they made me go, too, just to be certain I was okay.

Sitting up on the stretcher in the ambulance before they took me to the hospital, I could see Colleen Collins and her bodyguards getting back into the limo. The thin one seemed amused, in contrast with Colleen, who looked disappointed and frustrated.

The thin bodyguard opened the door for her, but before getting in, he turned his head toward the ambulance. I didn't know at first if he could see me through the windows, but he answered that question by smiling and giving me a slight nod. He had sent me a clear message: "We'll see you again."

It's YOUR Brain

The good news was that nothing was broken. I had a purple bruise in the shape of the bus door handle just below my right shoulder blade, but that was all.

The bad news was that my mom, who's an ER doctor, was on duty at the hospital when I was brought in. "Let me in there!" I could hear her demanding from the other side of the curtain.

"You have to let us finish up, Paige," my doctor said as he tried unsuccessfully to calm her.

"You already told me he's fine," my mom said, her voice steely. "Now let me in there so I can kill him."

The curtain flew aside and Mom pushed away the nurse who was testing my reflexes. She threw her arms around me and squeezed me with a hug that spoke volumes about how scared she must have been since hearing about the bus accident. The emotion of the moment was lost as her embrace made me spasm in pain.

"He has a pretty deep contusion on the upper back, Paige," the doctor warned. "You should probably be careful."

Mom wiped a tear from the side of her nose and regained her composure. "What's this I hear about you jumping out of a bus? What are you? Stupid? Are you trying to kill yourself?"

"I had to jump out or I would have fallen into the river *with* the bus."

"Why is it every other kid on the bus managed to get out just fine, but my son has to be the one who jumps out like he's trying to be a superhero?"

"He saved my life, ma'am," a weak voice answered from two beds away. The bus driver, his arm in a sling and his head dotted with stitches, tried to sit up a little straighter.

"What?" Mom's gaze bounced back and forth between me and the driver. "Who are you?"

"Al Mazzilli. I've been driving school buses for twenty-eight years and I've never had an accident until today. Everybody else was getting off the bus and forgot about me. I passed out, but then I see this kid trying to wake me up. He got me on my feet and got me out. Even gave me a kick in the butt when I needed it to get out the door."

Mom turned back to me and the tears started again despite her jaw's being set in "I am very angry" mode.

"You raised yourself a hero, ma'am," the bus driver told her. "I owe you one, kid."

o o o

Once all the paperwork had been completed and the doctors were sure I didn't have a concussion, Mom took me home. Dad warmed up dinner for both of us and sat at the table while we ate so he could get the whole story, which I dished out between mouthfuls of pasta.

"I wish I had made something better for dinner," he apologized. "You save a man's life and come home to spaghetti and sauce out of a jar. Not exactly a hero's welcome."

"At this point, I'll eat anything," I said.

"I'll make it up to you tomorrow," Dad promised. "We'll go out to eat—no, your mother works tomorrow. How about Thursday? Anywhere you want to go. Harlequin's?"

"Can we stop talking about food?" Mom inter-jected. "Aren't you the least bit concerned about what happened to your son today?"

"Sure," he assured her. "But the important thing is he's safe now. I saw everything on the news. They had footage from the traffic cam on the bridge. It looks like it was a freak accident."

"What do they think happened?" Mom asked.

"The accident investigator said black ice."

"Black ice?" my mom cried. "It was seventy degrees out!"

"What's black ice?" I asked.

"It's a thin layer of ice," my dad said. "It's so thin you can't see it, so you just see a regular black road."

"I don't buy it," Mom argued. "It must have been an oil spill. Or something went wrong with the bus's steering." She had a perfectly valid point. It had been a warm afternoon. Even if it hadn't been, it almost never got cold enough in Kanigher Falls for the roads to ice over. In the dead of winter, the lows might get down into the forties, but the temperature rarely dipped below freezing.

"I'm just telling you what the inspector said," Dad

reminded her. "If you want to argue about it, call him."

"Sorry," Mom sighed. "I'm just . . . It's been . . ." She exhaled deeply and let her head drop to the table in exhaustion.

"I couldn't have said it better," Dad said, taking her empty plate and kissing the top of her head.

o o o

I slept on my stomach, because whenever I rolled onto my back or my side, pain would tear through my bruise. Mom gave me one of the painkillers they'd prescribed at the hospital. The painkiller combined with my high-energy day to put me out in a matter of minutes.

Moments later, I opened my eyes and found myself on the bus again. Out the window I could read the sign to the Moldoff Bridge. Zach was telling me the difference between a cheeseburger and a hamburger with cheese.

"Watch out for ice!" I shouted to the driver as I leapt from my seat.

"Ice?" The driver laughed. "There's no ice."

No sooner had the words left his lips than we were spinning. Everyone screamed, but not in fear. They threw their arms into the air like riders on a roller coaster and screamed in excitement. The bus spun faster and faster until the world outside became a blur.

"Nightmares?" said a gruff voice from the front of the bus. Standing beside the driver was a large silhouette I couldn't quite make out.

Everything stopped, as though someone had hit pause on a DVD player, except I could still move, and so could the silhouette.

"Who are you?" I asked him, barely able to get the words out.

He stepped forward and my brain started to fill in details, turning him from a shadow into a large man in a midnight blue suit with a matching fedora and a thin black tie. He looked like a mobster from an old movie except for the blue cape that hung from his broad shoulders. His skin was dark and his features were hard, like he'd been carved from a piece of wood. Over his eyes, he wore a small domino mask. "I think you know who I am," he said with a deep southern accent.

"Doctor Nocturne?" I gasped. I had never seen the elusive Doctor Nocturne. There were no photographs of him, and the only people to describe him did so in confessions to police. Even so, when I saw him in my dream vision, I knew who he was immediately.

"That's what they call me." He gazed around the bus at the blurred surroundings. "Why don't we go somewhere else? You already went through this once today."

"Where should we go?"

"It's *your* brain. Think of someplace that makes you happy. It makes the connection easier."

The bus faded and suddenly we were standing together inside Funny Pages, my favorite comic-book store. "What is this?" Doctor Nocturne practically snarled at the racks of comic books. "I should have known you were into comics. No wonder the Ranger likes you so much."

"Who?"

"We'll talk about it later. In person. Making a telepathic connection like this ain't easy, especially when we're in different cities. That's why I had to wait until you were asleep."

"Wait. Am I dreaming all this or are you really here?" I asked. "And if I'm dreaming, how do I know I'm dreaming? Is that part of the dream?"

"Were you listening when I told you this wasn't easy?" he snapped. "Tomorrow night, we're going to have a little conversation, so I need you to come visit me. Understand?"

"You mean I'm going to dream about you again?" I asked, confused.

"No. I need you to come to me."

"But you live in Kurtzburg. That's two thousand miles east of here."

He grabbed a comic off the wall and opened it up. On the page he opened to, there was a big picture of a graveyard. The longer I looked at it, the more I felt myself drawn to it, until I realized I was standing on the soft cemetery grass. Doctor Nocturne pointed to a tomb at the top of a hill.

"See that mausoleum?" he asked. "Remember it."

I climbed the hill to get a better look. It was a small rectangular building carved out of white marble. On one of the narrow ends was a door with the name ZUEMBAY chiseled into it. "Where are we?"

"You need to go to Fawcett Memorial Lawns," he said. "Do you know how to get there?"

I'd never been inside, but I knew where Fawcett Memorial Lawns was. Every kid did. The legends said that Fawcett was haunted and that the dead walked the grounds at night. Halloween was coming up, and that meant dozens of kids would be daring one another to go inside and tie a scarf around a tree branch or leave some candy on a tombstone or do something to mark that they'd ventured more than twenty feet beyond the gates. Every year a few kids would take up the challenge, but every one of them would come running back out looking like the seat of his pants was on fire.

"I know where it is."

"Go there and find this mausoleum. Then we'll talk."

I ran my fingers into the carved Z on the door, but they slipped through. The door faded, along with the tomb, the hill, and all the grave markers, until I was floating in blackness without any ground to stand on. Doctor Nocturne had vanished. Details from the bus slowly began to return. The paused image of the bus spinning out of control materialized around me. As instantaneously as if someone had pressed play, the chaos resumed. The bus spun hundreds of times before shooting off the side of the bridge and plummeting thousands of feet into darkness.

Just a moment before the impact, I woke up drenched

in sweat, with my heart beating double time. I sat bolt upright, sending a lightning strike into the bruise on my back. I leaned over to my desk, found a pen, and scribbled the name *Zuembay* on the back of a piece of math homework.

Have You Ever Played Cribbage?

I spent the next day trying to decide whether my dream had been real. I wanted to tell Ms. Matthews about it, but she avoided me even more than she had for the past week.

Instead, I relied on the counsel of Fiona and Teddy.

"Are you crazy?" Teddy wheezed. "Doctor Nocturne doesn't live in Fawcett Lawns. Only ghosts live in there."

"You're just chicken," Fiona said accusingly. "I say we check it out."

"You really think Doctor Nocturne is going to be hanging out in a cemetery in Kanigher Falls?" I asked.

"No," she admitted. "I figure it was just a dream.

You probably hit your head in the bus and your brain was swelling, but just in case, let's see."

After dinner, I told my parents I was going to Teddy's to work on a history project. Teddy and Fiona told their parents they were coming to my house. We met in the middle of the road and set off for Fawcett Memorial Lawns.

"Remember Will Roberts? I heard he went into Fawcett Lawns on a dare last summer and he never came back out," Teddy told us as we rode our bikes the two miles to the cemetery. "The next day, the groundskeeper found a freshly dug grave and in it were Will's clothes and a pile of bones. The ghosts had eaten him alive."

"Will Roberts moved to a charter school," Fiona informed us. "He still plays third base on my Little League team."

"Besides, why would ghosts need to eat?" I said. "Now, if you had said werewolves, that might have made sense."

"Or vampires," Fiona added.

"No, vampires drink blood," I said, correcting her. "They don't eat people."

"They could!" Fiona argued.

"Guys, stop talking about this," Teddy pleaded.

"Oh, you know what would have been good?" Fiona added. "If a family of cannibals lived in the cemetery."

"Yeah!" I agreed enthusiastically. "And usually they eat the bodies that get buried each day, but when Will accidentally crossed their path, they were like, 'Jackpot!'"

"Guys!" Teddy begged.

This continued for the rest of the ride. Teddy threatened to turn back, but quickly realized he was more frightened to ride back alone than to stay with the group.

As we pulled up the driveway, the size of this task began to set in. There were no lights in the cemetery. We'd brought flashlights, but we still had several acres to cover on a dark, moonless night.

"What direction do you think we should head?" I asked.

"I don't suppose it really matters, does it?" Fiona said.

"This is going to take forever," I sighed.

"It's going to take even longer if we don't get started," she noted. "Pick a direction and go."

I swung my flashlight to the left and started down a path beside a pond full of ducks.

"Keep an eye out for—"

"Is that it?" Teddy asked. He pointed his flashlight up a small hill about five yards away. At the top of the hill was the mausoleum from my dream.

"Um, yeah," I confirmed.

We climbed the hill, and sure enough, the name ZUEMBAY was carved into the door.

"That was considerably easier than I expected," Fiona said. "Now where's Doctor Nocturne?"

We shone our flashlights on the tomb and into the surrounding trees, but didn't see anyone. We tried whispering, "Doctor Nocturne?" but got no reply.

"I think this proves your dream was just a dream," Teddy said. "Now how about we get out of here? We managed to come into Fawcett Lawns and not get attacked by the living dead—knock on wood—" He reached back and knocked superstitiously on the door to the Zuembay tomb.

"That's not wood, genius," Fiona scoffed.

"Whatever. The point is let's get out of here before—" He was interrupted when the door to the mausoleum slowly opened. Teddy stumbled backward into me and we both slipped to the ground and rolled down the hill. Fiona leapt backward, never turning her back on the door.

A bony hand reached out and held the door frame as the door swung fully open. We saw the shadow of a head and a pair of shoulders emerge. Fiona, being the only one still on her feet and somewhat composed, lifted her flashlight to illuminate the subject.

A skeletal face turned toward her, the flesh rotting and the eyes sunken so deeply into the sockets they seemed like empty pools of black. Its jaw hung slack and a low hissing escaped its throat.

"Hhhhhhchchchchch."

I don't remember running. I don't remember screaming. I don't remember falling into the duck pond. But since the next thing I remembered was screaming as I tried to get out of the duck pond, I have to assume all those things happened.

"Zombie!" Teddy cried. *"Zombie!"*

"Wwwwaaaaaaaaaahhhh!" the zombie yelled. "Nnnnaaaaaaaaaykhe!"

"Did he just say 'Nate'?" Fiona asked.

I didn't want to wait to find out. The zombie was lurching down the hill, now in pursuit. "Nooooo!" he yelled. "Doon' run away!"

I crawled out of the pond and bolted for the bikes, but they weren't where we had parked them. "Where did—"

Teddy shone his flashlight up into the branches of the willow tree near where we'd left our bikes. We could see a set of handlebars hanging above our heads. "How did they get—" Fiona began to ask when the tree answered that question for us, bringing its massive branches down around us and grabbing our arms and legs and holding us in place.

The zombie continued to run at us in a clumsy, off-balance fashion. The tree lifted us off the ground and held us firmly. At last, the zombie reached the base of the tree.

He put his hand firmly on his jaw. With a hard upward thrust, something popped. He stretched his mouth and moved his chin around as if testing it. "Sorry about that," he shouted up to us in a soft, gentle voice. "This jaw has been giving me trouble for about a week. I wish I could say I got into a scrape with

Wintertyrant or something cool like that, but no, I just fell down the stairs."

He waved one of his arms, and the tree gently lowered us and our bikes to the ground. "So, how about we try this again? What I was trying to say was 'Hey, you must be Nate.'" He extended a rotting hand covered in scabs. "I'm Captain Zombie."

I shook his hand carefully, afraid I might break it. "Capt—but you live in Haney."

"Well, I work in Haney. I live in the graveyard."

"The Haney graveyard?" Teddy squeaked.

"Among others. Why don't you guys follow me and I'll try to explain."

We went back up the hill to the tomb and followed him through the door and down a flight of marble stairs. At the bottom, the narrow staircase opened into a huge living room. A chandelier hung from the ceiling over a pool table, and in its light we got our first good look at Captain Zombie.

He certainly lived up to his name. Skin flaked off him, at least in the places where there was still skin. Wisps of hair clung to his scalp, but barely. When he picked up a can of soda to offer us a drink, the sinews in his hand could be seen tightening and retracting.

His teeth were brown and whenever he relaxed, his jaw would slacken and his mouth would hang wide open.

But he wore a satin jacket with black silk lounge pants and furry slippers, which was hardly a scary ensemble.

"Okay," Captain Zombie said, setting down a silver tray with three cans of soda and three glasses of ice. "I've heard of Nate Banks, but I'm afraid I'm not familiar with you two."

"I'm Fiona Wagner."

Teddy sat in a ball on a chair opposite Captain Zombie, looking almost on the verge of tears, but not saying anything.

"And this is Teddy Cochrane," Fiona continued. She shot Teddy in the ribs with an elbow. Nervously, he leaned forward and grabbed a glass and a can of soda.

"Oh, sorry about that!" Captain Zombie reached out and took Teddy's glass from him. He snaked a bony finger inside and fished out a yellow fingernail. "Guess I lost another one! Let me get you some clean ice."

Teddy retched silently and pulled his knees a little tighter to his chest.

"It's so great to have you guys here," Captain

Zombie said as he bounded to a marble bar to grab the ice bucket and tongs. "When Doctor Nocturne told me you were coming, I couldn't wait. I got out the cribbage board—have you ever played cribbage? I love cribbage—"

"Excuse me, Captain Zombie," I said. "I thought I was meeting with Doctor Nocturne."

"Oh, I'm sorry. Were you in a hurry? I just don't get guests very often, so I tend to get carried away."

"Is he coming here?"

"No, he hardly ever leaves Kurtzburg." He put his hands around his mouth like he was whispering gossip, but from across the room. "Though if you ask me, he should get out more often. Would do the old boy some good!"

"So how am I supposed to get to Kurtzburg?"

Captain Zombie pointed a finger at the entrance we'd come through. "Right up the stairs." He shuffled out from behind the bar, reaching into the pocket of his jacket. "Oh, I almost forgot. Here's some bus fare." Teddy started to get up, but Captain Zombie pushed him back into his seat, where he squirmed, much to Fiona's amusement. "You two wait here. Fiona, grab the cribbage board."

When we reached the top of the stairs, Captain Zombie pulled the door open. We stepped out onto the hill, but looking beyond the gates of the cemetery, I didn't recognize the skyline.

"Welcome to Kurtzburg," he said.

Living the Dream

There was a bus stop right outside the gate of the Kurtzburg Cemetery. Captain Zombie explained that his mausoleum existed simultaneously in every cemetery on the planet, which made him the go-to guy for quick transportation among the superhero set. He handed me the bus fare and told me to take the number seven bus. At the third stop, I was supposed to get off and meet Doctor Nocturne. "I'll be here when you get back," he promised.

On the bus, I counted the stops as I scanned the crowd, trying to get a good look at everyone, but afraid if I made eye contact, someone might interpret it the wrong way. There was an elderly woman coughing into a linty old tissue that she wadded up and shoved into her pocket. Three bandana-wearing guys covered in tattoos wore their pants around their thighs and seemed to be having a contest to see who could slump lowest in his seat. A man with a long, twisted beard picked something out of his hair, examined it, dropped it on the floor, and went digging for more. A woman in a waitress uniform sat with her left foot in her lap, rubbing her corns, her shoe on the seat beside her.

Well before the bus stopped for the third time, I leapt up and ran to the door. The bus dropped me on a street corner in an empty part of town. On just about any other night, I would have been terrified. Dark alleys offered the perfect hiding places for muggers, kidnappers, or worse. The streetlight at the bus stop flickered with a buzz reminiscent of a beehive and went out every few minutes, plunging the street into darkness.

But any fear I might have had at that point was overwhelmed by excitement. For more than half of my life, starting when I was only five, I'd been reading comic books. I could never begin to count the hours I'd spent reading them, rereading them, sealing them carefully in plastic bags with acid-free cardboard to prevent them from getting bent, and filing them alphabetically and numerically. Now I wasn't just reading someone else's made-up stories; I was living out the dream. Though it's safe to say most dreams don't involve standing on a deserted street corner on a cold October night in a city I'd never been to. Some nightmares, maybe, but not many dreams.

A man pushing a shopping cart with one bad wheel wobbled out of an alley and toward the bus stop. His cart was full of soda cans, a few blankets, and crumpled food wrappers. As he drew nearer, he cast a wary eye on me. "There was madness in any direction, at any hour," he muttered to himself. "You could strike sparks anywhere."

The closer he got, the less excited I was to be living the dream.

He came to a stop beside me and flung himself over the cart, shielding it from me. "Our energy would simply prevail," he whispered hoarsely. He sounded like a dog afraid I was going to take away its bone. Slowly, he turned the cart and headed down a side alley.

I turned back to the street and was startled to find a young woman standing next to me, just as the streetlight again went out. My surprised yelp couldn't find its way out of my throat. What dim light there was only helped to make this girl more mysterious. A fedora kept her face in shadow, though I could make out the edge of a small domino mask. A cape draped over her shoulders partially obscured her blue suit, which appeared to have been styled in the 1940s. It looked like something you'd see Franklin Roosevelt wearing, not a girl in her twenties from Kurtzburg. Her dark skin blended with the night.

"Who are you?" I asked cautiously.

"Who do you think I am?" she replied, extending her hand. "How many other superheroes invited you to Kurtzburg? I'm Doctor Nocturne."

"You looked different in my dream," I said as she shook my hand.

"I can see why Zilch said you were so clever," she responded drily. "Nothing gets by you, does it?"

"What I mean is Doctor Nocturne—"

"Is a man," she finished. "And an old one, at that. Yeah, I get that a lot. See, my dad—you know what? We'll explain all this at the mansion."

"Mansion?" I whispered.

"Follow me." She smiled mischievously.

She made her way down the closest alley, where

she'd left her motorcycle. In a flash, she put on her helmet and roared the slick machine to life. She pitched a matching helmet to me and jerked a thumb behind her, signaling me to jump on. No sooner had my butt touched the seat than we were tearing off down the road, making our way to the edge of town, where rocky cliffs overlooked Gerber Bay.

Her motorcycle wound down a narrow path and into a cave. We picked up speed, and I found the courage to look over her shoulder at where we were headed. All I could see was a wide, deep pit straight ahead. Without the slightest hesitation, she gunned the engine and jumped the motorcycle across the pit, landing with the back wheel only inches from the edge. I silently wondered how many bad guys trying to pursue her in the past had been lost at its bottom.

The motorcycle burst through a curtain of moss and weeds, putting us in a cavern full of high-tech computers and lab equipment that appeared to have been carved into the rocky walls. She parked the motorcycle and pulled off her helmet.

"Let's go upstairs." She gestured toward a hydraulic lift. "Dad's probably in the den waiting to talk to you."

I stepped into the small elevator and was shot up

through a narrow tube. My eardrums popped and my eyes felt like they were being pressed into the back of my skull while my stomach tried to escape into my feet and my legs struggled to keep me from crumpling into a heap.

It was the coolest ride ever.

When the elevator stopped, a door opened with a hiss. I leaned forward cautiously into a dark room that smelled familiar. I couldn't quite place the scent, but it reminded me of breakfast.

"French toast?" I whispered, sniffing deeply. As my eyes adjusted to the dark, I could see jars of nutmeg and cinnamon beside the elevator shaft. I was in a pantry. To my surprise, the hidden entrance to Doctor Nocturne's top secret lair was between a spice rack and a shelf full of cereal boxes.

"Are you planning to stand there all night?" a gruff voice asked from outside the pantry door. Startled, I stumbled out of the elevator and into the food cabinet, allowing the hydraulics to recede back down the shaft to bring up Doctor Nocturne. I reached out and turned the handle to the cabinet door, opening the entrance to a dimly lit kitchen. Leaning on a cane was a large gray-haired man wearing what seemed to be a permanent scowl. "You sure took your time," he grumbled before raising a glass of iced tea to his mouth and emptying it.

I recognized the voice from my dream, though he looked a bit different. He hobbled forward, leaning on the cane with every other step. With the exception of the limp, he appeared to be healthy and strong. His gray hair and weathered face made me guess he was in his late fifties or early sixties, but his powerful build, barrel chest, and muscular arms would have been the envy of men in their twenties.

"Doctor Nocturne?" I asked.

A Monkey Could Get a B in Art Class!

"Nate Banks," Doctor Nocturne said, not asking or confirming but stating it as though he was telling me that would be my name whether he was correct or not. "How do you get a D in art class?"

"Excuse me?"

He picked up from the kitchen counter a file folder with my name written across it in marker. "Last spring you got a D in art class. What did you do? Try to eat your macaroni painting? A monkey could get a B in junior high school art class!"

"Well, it's complicated—" I started to explain.

"No, it's not," he barked. "You just don't apply yourself."

I wasn't sure what to say. In the past half hour, I'd gone from a mausoleum in a graveyard in Kanigher

Falls to a street two thousand miles away to a spice-filled pantry in a stranger's kitchen. And now I was being berated for my lackluster scholastic record. My brain was having a little trouble soaking it all in.

"Boy, fighting supervillains is a whole lot harder than making a papier-mâché donkey —"

"It was supposed to be a rabbit," I corrected him, but he just glared at me. He held up a photo of a pile of wet newsprint that didn't resemble a donkey, a rabbit, or any other member of the animal kingdom. He gestured at the photo.

"If this is too much for you, I don't think it's going to make much sense to let you put yourself in a situation where you can cross paths with Terrorantula or Devast-8."

"Calm down, Dad," the younger Doctor Nocturne chimed in as she entered from the pantry door behind me.

"I'm not going to be calm," he insisted. "How calm do you think the media is going to be when this boy who can't even maintain a C-minus average in the sixth grade makes some stupid decision that gets him crushed by Colosso? How calm do you think the government is going to be when they find out a kid who doesn't know how to write a remainder in decimals is responsible for keeping Kanigher Falls from being taken over by alien invaders?"

The younger Doctor Nocturne smiled sheepishly at me. She raised her eyebrows slightly as she removed her mask, as if both to apologize for her father's outburst and to express the understanding of someone who'd been on this end of several others in her lifetime. "Hi, Nate. I'm Stephanie Duncan, but everybody calls me Steph. This is my dad—"

"Everybody calls me Doctor Nocturne," he insisted. "I've looked at everything in this file three times, and I can't understand why you're here."

Steph stood at the open fridge, pouring herself a glass of lemonade. She raised the pitcher to offer me some. I shook my head politely, afraid of provoking her father.

"It doesn't matter what's in the file," she told him. "What matters is that he's here, so let's get on with this so I can get him back to the graveyard and get back on patrol."

He walked past me down a hallway, continuing to talk. I followed, assuming that was what he expected. "Sophie Matthews, junior high school social studies teacher. How did she choose that secret identity?"

"I don't think she chose it as a secret identity," I speculated. "I think she just wanted to be a teacher."

"Well, it's not very convenient for a superhero," he said disapprovingly. "Staff meetings, detention, the set bell schedule—all things that can impede one's crime fighting. She'd be better off as a reporter or a private detective or self-employed. That makes it much easier to get away at a moment's notice."

"She manages," I replied.

"So far." We arrived in a living room that could have doubled as a football stadium in a pinch, though it was lit by just one dim lamp. My host sat in a large leather chair. Stephanie unhooked her cape from her shoulders, draped it over the arm of the luxurious sofa, and sat beside it. "Please have a seat," Doctor Nocturne said, gesturing toward the empty couch and chairs, his booming baritone voice echoing in the cavernous room.

I sank into a chair and examined the two people across from me. "The cane," I blurted, pointing at it resting against the chair. "Now it makes sense. You've recently injured yourself and had to pass on the Doctor Nocturne mantle to your daughter. I've been trying to figure out how a girl in her twenties could have been fighting Red Malice in the 1950s — "

"And been a man," Stephanie added.

"Right! And been a man, according to every eyewitness account for more than fifty years. So what do you do? Pass off the costume every ten years or so? How many Doctor Nocturnes have there been?"

"Just the two of us," the elder Doctor Nocturne answered.

"How can that be? The first reports of Doctor Nocturne surfaced around 1954. That would make you seventy, maybe eighty years old."

The man's mouth pinched into a sour expression, but his daughter laughed. "Looks like you're not the only one with a file," she told her father.

"Your math is a little off, but that's to be expected, since you're missing some information," the man in the chair noted. "I'll be eighty-nine next month."

My logic train screeched to a halt. This man looked barely older than my father, but he claimed he was old enough to be my grandfather's father.

"And I appreciate you calling me 'a girl in her twenties,'" his daughter added. "But I'm forty-seven."

The senior Doctor Nocturne chuckled. I assumed it was because he had retaken the upper hand in this conversation. "We've gotten sidetracked. I had intended for this to be a fairly quick conversation. I understand you want to be a sidekick to Ultraviolet—"

"Not so much a sidekick," I corrected him. "More of an advisor."

He didn't seem to care for my distinction. "Personally, I think this is a mistake. I have to admit that rescuing that bus driver was pretty impressive, and you held up really nicely when that Malcontent guy used you as a shield—"

"Thanks."

"But there's a lot more to this business than being in the wrong place at the wrong time. You've been lucky, but eventually luck runs out. See, your problem is that you jump into situations without looking at all the pieces of the puzzle. You need to learn to stop and focus and figure out what you're getting yourself into before you get yourself killed. I don't think you have that in you."

"The thing is," his daughter chimed in, obviously trying to head off his heavy-handed attack, "Phantom Ranger himself asked that Ultraviolet give you a chance to prove yourself, and that we help."

"Phantom . . . R-Ranger?" I gasped. "H-he was talking about me?"

"I guess so," said the old man. "All I do know is that he thinks there's something inside that head of yours that doesn't show up in this file. What you have going for you is that I learned a long time ago that when Phantom Ranger says something, you ought to listen."

A smile broke out on my lips, but I hurried to suppress it before Doctor Nocturne snapped at me.

"Before you get too excited, there are a few conditions. Come Christmas break, you'd better be floating on a B average, and that's just a start. I'm going to keep an eye on you, boy. Any questions?"

With all the details still sorting themselves out in my head, I wasn't sure what I'd agreed to. But there was one thing that came to mind as Stephanie, back in her Doctor Nocturne outfit, and I made our way to the pantry exit. "How can you be forty-seven?"

o o o

As I opened the door to the mausoleum, the first thing I heard was Teddy sobbing. Quickly, I ran down the stairs to find him curled up in a ball in his chair. Fiona was howling as well, while Captain Zombie stood in the middle of the room with a crazy smile plastered on his decrepit face. Teddy sat up and wiped tears from his eyes, but it quickly became apparent they weren't from crying.

"Wait, it gets better," Captain Zombie told them through laughs. "So Demonica is trying to summon her powers, going through this whole incantation, and I'm just waiting, because I figure I'll give her a scare. Anyway, she finishes up and does one of these numbers—" He thrust both hands out in front of him as if he was casting a spell.

"Nothing happens?" Fiona guessed.

"Nothing happens!" Captain Zombie confirmed, and all three of them went into a giggling fit. "Then I summon up a little of the ol' Power of the Graveyard and have a few skeletal hands pop up out of the ground and start dragging her down."

"Nate, you're back," Teddy said, finally noticing me.

"I guess you guys had a good time."

"Dude, cribbage is the best game!" Teddy told me.

"Oh, and try this brisket," Fiona offered, holding up a Styrofoam box full of meat slathered in barbecue sauce. "Captain Zombie had it delivered from Haney."

"Best barbecue on the planet. Next time you guys come by, we'll get some real deep-dish pizza from Weisinger," Captain Zombie promised. "One of the advantages of simultaneously existing everywhere. How was your meeting?"

"It was . . . um . . . good, I guess." I wasn't quite sure how to classify it. I'd gotten good news, but the way it had been delivered made me feel like I'd been caught playing football next to Mom's china hutch.

"Doctor Nocturne came off as kind of a jerk, didn't he?" Captain Zombie asked sympathetically.

I nodded reluctantly.

"He's not that bad," Captain Zombie assured me. "He's having a little trouble coping with the injury and giving up the uniform. He's been out fighting crime on the streets for more than sixty years. He needs a little time to adjust."

Teddy and Fiona grudgingly got out of their seats and shook Captain Zombie's hand, promising to be back soon.

"And, Teddy, remember what I said about that

Allison girl," he shouted after us as we walked back up the stairs. "She'll come around. You just have to get her attention. You've got to find a way to be a big shot and save the day without coming off as arrogant. Trust me, when the time is right, you'll know."

Fiona rolled her eyes and muttered, "They talked about her the entire time they played cribbage."

The Ugliest Snowmen I'd Ever Seen

If I expected any recognition of my Phantom Ranger seal of approval from Ms. Matthews, I was going to be disappointed. The entire day passed without so much as a word from her. Not a "Welcome aboard," or an "If Phantom Ranger believes in you, so do I," or even an "I really hate this idea!"

Dad made good on his offer, taking us out to dinner at Harlequin's. Mom was meeting us there, but first Dad had to stop at the bank to deposit a check.

While Dad waited in line, my sister, Denise, and I stayed at the small desk near the back of the lobby. I killed time by doodling on a deposit slip with a pen attached to a chain. In my drawing, Nightowl was lurking in the box labeled CURRENCY while his arch-nemesis, Dr. Jackal, climbed up the check registry.

I picked up the pen and examined my drawing. It was pretty bad, even without the bank's watermark making Nightowl's boot look twice as wide as I'd meant it to.

"I can't tell whether you're just a terrible artist or if Mom and Dad should get your eyes examined," Denise scoffed.

A cool breeze whipped past and blew the deposit slip onto the ground. My first thought was that the air conditioner had suddenly kicked on, and I instinctively looked up to find the vent. But the breeze grew colder and more intense, and it wasn't coming from the vents in the ceiling.

Standing in the doorway was a thin man wearing a shiny blue suit with silver pinstripes and a pair of blue sunglasses. He looked like he'd been standing in the middle of a blizzard. His hair and goatee were covered in millions of tiny ice crystals, with some extending into long icicle-like spikes, and his skin had the blue tinge of someone who'd frozen to death.

The difference was that people who have frozen to death don't smile as broadly as he was. And they don't yell things like "Get on the floor, everybody. This is a holdup!"

I'd seen that face enough times on the news. "Coldsnap," I mouthed silently to my sister as we lay on the cool tile floor.

"Duh, you think?" she whispered.

Coldsnap was a supervillain who, as his name implied, could manipulate the temperature around him by freezing things with the snap of his fingers. He'd last been seen in Darwyn City, where he'd frozen the foundation of the Schigiel Building and brought the entire building to the ground. But that had been just six months earlier. There was no reason he should have been out of prison yet, and there hadn't been anything in the news about a jailbreak.

Dad held out an open palm and stared at us with intense eyes, a signal I clearly understood to mean "Even though there's a supervillain here to rob the bank, everything's going to be okay as long as we don't do anything stupid. So don't do anything stupid."

Coldsnap walked calmly toward the tellers, keeping his empty hands up and to the sides so they were in plain sight at all times. "This should be fairly easy," he promised. "I'm just going to make a quick withdrawal, and no one has to get hurt." With each step, a sheet of ice formed on the tile beneath his feet.

A man who'd been a few people in front of my dad in line casually reached for his cell phone and began dialing with his thumb as subtly as he could. Coldsnap pointed his left hand at the man and snapped the fingers on his right hand. A blast of snow surrounded the man's hand and phone, causing him to shriek.

"What I said was no one *has* to get hurt. If you want to lose a few fingers to frostbite, that's up to you. I'm more than willing to oblige."

The head teller opened the door to let Coldsnap into the back. He immediately set to rifling through the tellers' drawers. When I saw that, I breathed a relieved sigh. I knew from reading lots of comic books that each teller's drawer had an alarm in it. The bill on the bottom of the stack of fives was usually held in place by a small clip. If that bill was pulled from the drawer, the clip would close an electric circuit and set off an alarm at the police station.

"Let me guess," Coldsnap said to the bank manager as he gestured toward the door to the vault. "You keep this thing locked and there's no way you can open it, right?"

The frightened manager nodded hesitantly.

"Don't worry about it," Coldsnap said. He snapped his fingers with both hands, then pressed them against the huge vault door. A thin layer of ice coated the door. Small cracks began to form in the ice almost immediately. The bolts and rivets that held the door together snapped. The temperature in the bank had dropped enough that clouds of mist rose from the mouths of all the customers lying on the floor whenever we exhaled.

Finally, the vault door burst, a slurry of ice and snow oozing from the massive crack across its middle. A swift kick from Coldsnap and the inner door fell away, allowing the criminal to climb inside and loot the stacks of cash inside.

While Coldsnap was in the vault, my dad pulled himself quickly across the floor on his elbows. "Don't worry, kids," he said, trying to comfort us. "The police will be here soon. Breaking open the vault door like that's going to trigger an alarm."

I figured the same thing. I hoped Ultraviolet had also gotten the message.

Coldsnap emerged from the vault, with large-denomination bills sticking from every pocket in his suit, just in time to hear police sirens.

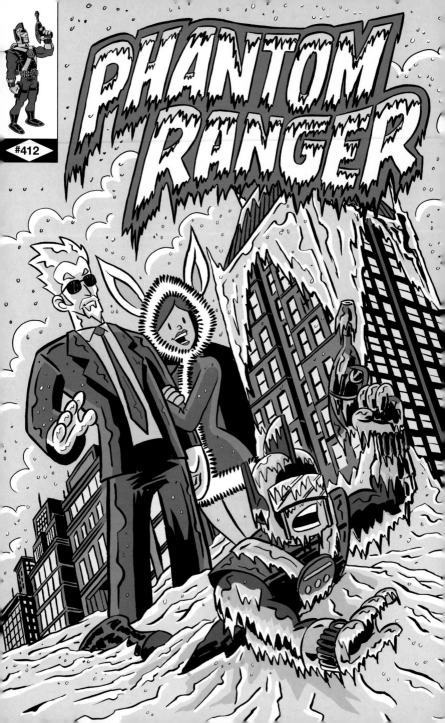

THERE ARE THREE TYPES OF CRIMES.

CRIMES OF PREMEDITATION ARE THOSE YOU PLAN AHEAD OF TIME.

SHUNK!

LIKE WHEN YOU CAREFULLY MONITOR AN ARMORED CAR'S DAILY ROUTINE SO YOU CAN SPRING THE PERFECT TRAP TO ROB IT.

CRIMES OF PASSION ARE UNPLANNED AND COMMITTED IN AN OVERLY EMOTIONAL STATE.

ZZAP!

ZZAP!

LIKE WHEN YOU GET SO MAD THAT SOME DO-GOODER LIKE THE PHANTOM RANGER RUINS YOUR PERFECT PLAN THAT YOU DO SOMETHING RASH.

HOLD IT RIGHT THERE, COLDSNAP!

CRIMES OF OPPORTUNITY ARE THE ONES YOU NEVER EVEN *THINK* OF COMMITTING...

...UNTIL THE *OPPORTUNITY* FALLS RIGHT INTO YOUR LAP.

WELL? ARE YOU JUST GOING TO **STARE** AT IT ALL DAY, OR ARE YOU GOING TO **TRY IT ON?**

I'M NOT SURE IF I SHOULD.

WHAT'S THE MATTER? YOU **AFRAID?**

OF COURSE I'M NOT AFRAID, SNOWBUNNY.

I WOULD JUST LIKE TO KNOW EXACTLY WHAT WE'RE DEALING WITH BEFORE I START PLAYING WITH IT.

HAVE YOU SEEN SOME OF THAT EQUIPMENT THE PHANTOM RANGER HAS?

FOR ALL WE KNOW, I MIGHT USHER IN A NEW ICE AGE WITH THIS THING.

THEN LET'S START SMALL.

"HOW ABOUT THAT LITTLE VAULT JOB AT THE SCHIGIEL BUILDING YOU'VE BEEN TALKING ABOUT?"

I CAN SENSE THE WATER MOLECULES ON THE OTHER SIDE OF THIS DOOR.

I JUST CAN'T GET THEM TO FREEZE TOGETHER.

I WAS HOPING I'D HAVE MORE TIME TO EXPERIMENT WITH THIS BEFORE I USED IT.

QUIT STALLING AND DO IT!

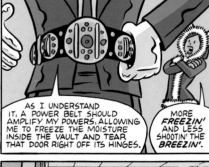

AS I UNDERSTAND IT, A POWER BELT SHOULD AMPLIFY MY POWERS, ALLOWING ME TO FREEZE THE MOISTURE INSIDE THE VAULT AND TEAR THAT DOOR RIGHT OFF ITS HINGES.

MORE *FREEZIN'* AND LESS *SHOOTIN'* THE *BREEZIN'*.

THERE ARE NO *LABELS* ON THESE DIALS. I'M NOT SURE WHAT THEY EVEN *DO*.

ONLY ONE WAY TO FIND OUT!

FREEZE, COLDSNAP!

THE RANGER WAS RIGHT. I DIDN'T KNOW WHAT I WAS DEALING WITH.

I TURNED UP THE POWER BELT TOO HIGH AND I COULDN'T CONTROL IT.

AND THAT'S HOW I WOUND UP HERE.

THEY'RE MAKING ME WEAR THESE POWER DAMPENERS BECAUSE MY POWERS HAVE BEEN KIND OF... *UNPREDICTABLE* SINCE THEN.

SO, YOU SAID YOUR CLIENT COULD GET ME OUT OF HERE.

WITHOUT GOING INTO TOO MUCH DETAIL, MY CLIENT HAS... INFLUENCE.

I'VE BEEN ORDERED TO GET THE CHARGES DISMISSED AND HAVE YOU BACK ON THE STREETS WITHIN TWELVE HOURS.

PERSONALLY I'M AIMING FOR SEVEN.

UH-HUH. WHAT'S THE CATCH?

MY CLIENT ONLY ASKS THAT YOU DO A JOB FOR HER IN KANIGHER FALLS.

ARE YOU FAMILIAR WITH THE SUPERHERO ULTRAVIOLET?

I'VE HEARD A COUPLE OF GUYS IN HERE MENTION THE NAME. THEY SAY SHE'S STRONG-- REAL POWERFUL.

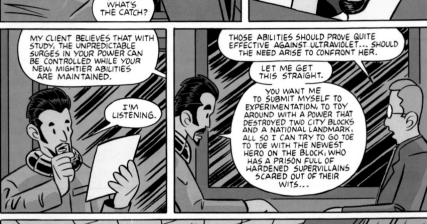

MY CLIENT BELIEVES THAT WITH STUDY, THE UNPREDICTABLE SURGES IN YOUR POWER CAN BE CONTROLLED WHILE YOUR NEW, MIGHTIER ABILITIES ARE MAINTAINED.

I'M LISTENING.

THOSE ABILITIES SHOULD PROVE QUITE EFFECTIVE AGAINST ULTRAVIOLET... SHOULD THE NEED ARISE TO CONFRONT HER.

LET ME GET THIS STRAIGHT.

YOU WANT ME TO SUBMIT MYSELF TO EXPERIMENTATION, TO TOY AROUND WITH A POWER THAT DESTROYED TWO CITY BLOCKS AND A NATIONAL LANDMARK, ALL SO I CAN TRY TO GO TOE TO TOE WITH THE NEWEST HERO ON THE BLOCK, WHO HAS A PRISON FULL OF HARDENED SUPERVILLAINS SCARED OUT OF THEIR WITS...

WHERE DO I SIGN?

"Hey, what do you know? I guess there is a police department in this town after all." He looked at his watch and scoffed. "Seven minutes? That's embarrassing."

He hustled to the front door. My dad threw one arm over me and the other around Denise, pulling us close to shield us.

"Folks, it's been great fun working with you all today," Coldsnap told us. "I know it may seem like we're done here, but I'm going to have to ask you all to stay on the floor a little bit longer. If experience has taught me anything in situations like these, it's that there will probably be some bullets flying around here very shortly, and the safest place you can be is right where you are."

He smiled crookedly and gazed at us over the top of his glasses. "Incidentally, the most dangerous place you can be is sneaking up behind me, trying to play hero while I'm making my escape. We cool?"

Standing at the front door, Coldsnap stretched his arms, legs, and neck like he was limbering up to run a race. "Stay cool. Stay cool," he muttered to himself.

The customers on the floor—my dad, Denise, and I included—shuffled nervously, trying to find something to hide behind that was heavy enough to stop a bullet yet still afforded a view of the action out the front door. Dad and I huddled behind a pillar near the new-customer sign-in desk while Denise slipped behind a filing cabinet. The pillar was about three feet wide and made of solid plaster. By leaning just slightly to my right, I could see everything that was happening.

Coldsnap snapped his fingers on both hands, then held his palms facing each other about a foot apart. An ice cube formed between them, levitating on an arctic breeze. He scrunched his face up in concentration, and the ice grew until he had something the size of a beach ball between his hands.

The icy wind blew open the doors while the ball of ice continued to swell. Three police cars were parked outside the bank, and six officers crouched behind the cars, only their heads and their guns visible.

"Coldsnap," one shouted into a megaphone, "there's nowhere to run. Come out with your hands up!"

"Oh, I knew that was coming," Coldsnap laughed, throwing his hands into the air. When he did, the chunk of ice—which was now the size of a large boulder—rolled forward, bounding down the bank steps and smashing into two of the police cars. The robber then snapped his fingers again, instantly forming an ice barrier around his entire body. It was several inches thick and covered him from head to toe, but cracks speckled it as soon as it was in place. It took me a moment to realize they were from police gunshots.

My dad pulled me back behind the pillar just as Coldsnap gave his shield a hard shove. I leaned out far enough to see it fly into the third cop car, sending the police ducking for cover. Coldsnap walked out onto the top step and surveyed the sky. The police started to regroup, and he looked at them with annoyance.

What we didn't realize while we were inside was that during the entire robbery, it had been snowing pretty heavily outside the bank. That in itself was remarkable, considering that the last time it had snowed in Kanigher Falls had been in 1926. To make matters even stranger, it wasn't the pretty kind of snow that blankets the world in a peaceful scene of white, like you see on Christmas cards. Coldsnap's snow was slushy and slightly brownish. And it smelled bad. Like rotten cabbage.

At first I thought the snow was just a side effect of

Coldsnap's being in the building, but I quickly realized it was more than that. It was part of his plan.

While the police relayed tactical plans to one another and kept a careful eye on Coldsnap, they never looked behind them. The blanket of snow rippled to life. Suddenly, the flakes flowed together to form a series of mounds. The taller the mounds got, the more detail they took on.

Soon five of the ugliest snowmen I'd ever seen stood silently behind the police.

The dirty, mushy snow that had fallen on the street and the grass had come together — along with some sticks for arms and some stones for eyes and mouths — to form a looming support team for Coldsnap. Just when the police gave the signal to spring their counteroffensive on the bank robber, Coldsnap snapped his fingers and the snowmen swarmed.

Two officers were engulfed in brown mush and dragged to the ground. Another was slammed into the door of one of the damaged cars.

I stepped out from behind the pillar and took a few steps forward to get a better view. My dad didn't bother to pull me back for my own safety. In fact, the scene was so bizarre he was advancing toward the door himself.

The remaining officers tried to fight the snowmen, but found their batons pummeling wet snow and doing no damage. "We need backup!" one screamed into his radio as a slow-moving mound of slush oozed over him, the snowman's mouth of pebbles twisting into a wicked grin.

Another cop smashed the head of a snowman into a spray of ice crystals and stones. Unfortunately, it took only a few seconds for the head to re-form. The cop quickly found himself on the ground, soaked in filthy, icy water.

With the police occupied, Coldsnap strolled casually down the stairs and toward an ice cream truck that had been parked by the curb with the engine running.

He spun around just in time to see Ultraviolet descending from the sky in a blur, her fist cocked to deliver a knockout blow.

With a chuckle, he snapped his fingers.

A block of ice crashed to the street beside the ice cream truck with a tremendous thud. Ultraviolet was encased within the frozen mass.

Coldsnap leapt into the truck and peeled away.

By now, most of us in the bank were standing in the doorway, staring at the frozen mass in the road. It took only seconds for cracks to form in the ice block and for Ultraviolet to shatter it into a cloud of snowflakes and tiny ice shards, but it seemed much longer. Brushing the remaining ice from her costume and hair, she glanced around as if trying to make sense of where she was, or maybe where Coldsnap was.

She spotted me instead of the supervillain. A perplexed look flashed briefly across her face. I flew into action, pointing wildly in the direction Coldsnap had gone. "He went that way, Ultraviolet!" I shouted clearly and boldly.

She nodded and took to the air, disappearing in a streak of purple and white.

Dad's hand landed on my shoulder. His eyes surveyed the chaos and he took a deep, worried breath.

"Do you think we'll be able to get away with not telling your mother about this?"

Information I Might Not Want a Supervillain to Know

The ice cream truck sat empty with one of its front wheels up on the curb and the driver's-side door hanging open as though someone had made a quick exit. A hole about the size of a fist—a purple-gloved fist, I guessed—was punched in the side of the van, right through a picture of a red, white, and blue Popsicle.

"By the time police arrived on the scene you see behind me, Ultraviolet had already found the stolen ice cream truck," a reporter said as the camera zoomed out to include him in the shot. "But there was no trace of Coldsnap, save for a note left on the driver's seat. Police told us it read 'Do you really think I'm stupid enough to make a getaway in something this obvious?' Wherever Coldsnap has gone, police have no leads. I guess you could say the trail has gone . . . *cold.* This is Chip Hardin reporting for *Channel Six News Now.*"

Unfortunately, the trail wasn't the only thing that had gone cold. I shivered under a blanket on the couch while my dad cooked oatmeal in the kitchen. Normally, I hate oatmeal, but our house was freezing. The idea of spackling my innards with piping-hot paste was too tempting to pass up.

My first clue that something was amiss had been when I'd had to push aside four blankets to roll out of bed. Mom had woken up in the middle of the night to find that the temperature outside had dropped below freezing. Overnight lows in Kanigher Falls were normally around sixty in October, so we hadn't even bothered to turn on the heater. My mom fired up the heat, but, knowing it would take hours to warm the house, she had had no choice but to empty the linen closet and cover my sister and me in thick cocoons of spare blankets.

As soon as I had thrown aside the mass of blankets, I wanted to crawl back under them. I could see my breath as I sat on the edge of the bed, shivering. I darted to my dresser and threw on the warmest clothes I could find, but even a sweatshirt and jeans didn't do much to block out the cold. When I went to brush my teeth, no water came out of the tap, and when I flushed the toilet, the tank didn't refill.

"The pipes are frozen, genius," Denise sneered when she walked by and saw me jiggling the toilet handle.

And worst of all, Coldsnap's snow, which lay in clumps all across the neighborhood—and, as I'd learn as the day wore on, the whole city—stunk. It reminded me of boiled hot dogs.

Before eating Dad's oatmeal, I held my frozen face over the bowl, letting the steam thaw it.

"Record lows for Kanigher Falls overnight," the weatherman on the morning news said. "Thirty degrees reported at the airport right now. That's well below our previous record of forty-six, recorded waaaaay back in 1938. Now, for a look at traffic and some warnings about icy road conditions, let's go up to Sky6 and our own Cap'n Norm."

I spooned brown sugar onto the oatmeal while Cap'n Norm, the station's helicopter pilot, ran through a list of road closures while hovering above the Moldoff Bridge and pointing out the gridlocked traffic for the camera. After my sixth scoop of sugar, my dad silently pushed the canister to the side without looking away from the television. I couldn't understand why he bothered watching, though, since every time he sipped his coffee, a puff of fog would appear on his glasses, obscuring his view.

"Of course, this unseasonably cold weather is believed to have a very simple explanation," the booming news anchor's voice said. "Returning to our top story, temperatures have been consistently dropping since yesterday's robbery of the Kanigher Falls Credit Union by supervillain Coldsnap, leading police to suspect the criminal may still be somewhere in town."

The TV showed choppy, pixelated security-camera footage of Coldsnap breaking open the vault. Then the anchor cut to an interview with the chief of police.

"This looks bad, but it really could have been worse," the chief said from the front steps of the bank. "Fortunately, the perpetrator chose a fairly small institution and was only able to abscond with a minimal amount of cash, due in no small part to a series of security measures that alerted the police immediately."

"That's a good plan," my dad sighed. "Tell the super-villain who's obviously still in town that he robbed a bank that was too small, and that he did a sloppy job. Why not just invite him to pull a heist downtown at one of the major bank branches?"

Dad and the chief were both right. I was surprised by what a bad job Coldsnap had done. I was just a twelve-year-old kid, but I'd seen enough cop shows and read enough comics to know about the alarm triggers in teller drawers and vaults. Coldsnap was a career criminal who'd robbed more banks than I could count. How did he not know that a small credit union branch on the north side of town would have only a fraction of the amount of cash on hand that—

Then it hit me.

He *had* known.

And he'd wanted the police to come. What was more, he had wanted Ultraviolet to come.

This wasn't about money. If it had been, he would have been long gone. This was a direct challenge to Ultraviolet. But why?

I shoveled in the last few bites of the oatmeal–brown sugar concoction I'd mixed in my bowl, threw on a jacket, and took off for school, determined to find out.

o o o

I didn't have to look very hard to find Ms. Matthews. She was already looking for me.

"I saw you at the bank yesterday," she muttered under her breath as we walked the hallway back to her classroom. "What were you doing there?"

"What was I—I was drawing a picture on a deposit slip while my dad waited to cash a check. Why does it matter why I was there?"

"I'm sorry. It was just a bit of a coincidence is all," she said. "I was afraid maybe you knew ahead of time."

"And you thought if I knew, I'd go volunteer to be a hostage in a shoot-out just so I could see Coldsnap in person?"

Ms. Matthews shrugged slightly.

"Okay," I admitted. "That does sound like something I *might* do . . . but I didn't!"

Once we reached the classroom, she closed the door behind us, glancing into the hallway one last time to make sure we wouldn't be bothered. "Did you notice anything inside the bank? Did he say anything that might give us a hint as to why he didn't leave town after he got away? Why stick around if the job's done?"

"He didn't rob the bank for the money," I said. "He

did it to get your attention. He set off the alarms on purpose. He didn't bother even filling a bag with cash. He only took what would fit in his pockets. He wanted a fight, and he wanted to show Kanigher Falls that he could beat Ultraviolet."

As soon as I said it, another thought occurred to both of us.

"The bus," Ms. Matthews said.

"He laid down the ice thinking Ultraviolet would come save us." I was starting to put the pieces together. "When you didn't change into your uniform, he had to come up with a new plan—the bank."

"Now I have to figure out what his next plan is going to be," Ms. Matthews said. She coughed and scrunched up her nose. "What is that smell?"

I took a deep whiff and gagged. "It's from the snow. I don't know what's wrong with it, but it stinks."

We looked out the window at the beige flakes that fell from the sky. The snowfall had become heavier, and I couldn't help sensing that that was a bad thing.

The bell rang and everyone rushed to class, but just as the halls became thickest with students, the power went out. I had just been about to leave Ms. Matthews's classroom so I could get to math, but I decided against it when I saw the darkened hallway. At least the windows kept the classroom bright enough to see, even without the fluorescent lights overhead.

I looked out the window and saw Coldsnap standing in the courtyard without any fear of being noticed. He raised his arms like a conductor calling an orchestra to order. With each little gesture, the snow on the ground rippled with a life of its own. "Looks like it's a little late to figure out what his next plan is," I said.

"He's on to me," Ms. Matthews concluded. "He must know my identity. That's why he attacked the bus; that's why he's here now. I'd better get out there. I'm just endangering everyone as long as I stay in here." She started for the door, but I stopped her.

"No," I said, realizing something. "It's not you. It's me."

"What?"

"You weren't at the bank; I was. He's been following me and putting me in danger, because he thinks that's the way to get you to respond. He thinks you're keeping an eye on me."

"And why would he think that?" she asked with a note of annoyance. "Maybe it's because someone told him—and anyone else who would listen—that you were my trusted sidekick?"

"I'm not a sidekick; I'm an *advisor.* But yes, now that you mention it, that does seem like information I might not want a supervillain to know."

I could tell that Ms. Matthews wanted to yell at me right then and there, but some other students suddenly began filing into the room. They weren't in her class, but they were taking advantage of a chance to get out of the dark hallways.

Coldsnap lowered his left arm, snapped his fingers, and raised his arm again. Behind him, the snow responded, forming a wall at least fifteen feet high. He repeated the action with his right arm, then swung both toward the school. The two juggernauts of frozen brown slush lumbered forward, gaining momentum until they crashed into the side of the building.

The impact shattered a few windows and knocked several people off their feet. The walls of wretched, filthy, stinking snow completely covered the windows, plunging the classrooms into the same darkness as the halls. More shudders rocked the building farther down, closer to the science classrooms, and though we couldn't see him any longer, we knew that Coldsnap was sealing off the building completely.

"You need to get out," I whispered to Ms. Matthews. "If Ultraviolet doesn't show up, there's no telling what he'll do."

I couldn't see her face in the dark, but I knew she was reluctant to leave a classroom full of students at a time like this. But she also knew that only Ultraviolet could stop this, so she carefully crept out of the room and down the dark halls to find an exit.

Meanwhile, I began digging. After sweeping aside the shattered glass from the windows that now oozed with mush that stunk of old vegetables, I scooped armfuls of the muck into the classroom, trying to tunnel out. Unfortunately, the snow was so watery, it sank in on itself instead of staying packed to form a tunnel.

After three tries, I managed to get a single beam of sunlight to break through, illuminating the room for about a second before the snow collapsed and sealed us back in. But if one big scoop could break through to the sun, the wall of snow couldn't be more than a few feet thick.

I crouched in front of the broken window and took

a deep breath. I stretched my arms in front of me as far as I could make them reach, then plunged them both into the snow. One of my hands managed to wriggle free on the other side, which made me think my plan might just work. After another long, deep breath, I pulled as much snow through the hole as I could, leaving an alcove with a hole about the size of a dinner plate on the other side. With all the power my legs could give me, I dove toward that sunlight like a swimmer plunging into a pool.

Both hands made it through, but then the rest of the wall dropped in on me. As hundreds of pounds of snow collapsed onto the yellowing bruise across my back, the pain made me question my brilliant plan. The weight of the snow crushed every inch of my body, squeezing me like hundreds of frozen pythons. The cold tore through my skin, numbing every part of my body. While I was slowly losing feeling from the outside in, I also noticed a burning in my mouth, nose, and eyes. The mushy brown snow was laced with salt—which explained why it wasn't freezing correctly—that soaked into all the soft tissue on my face. It seeped into a scratch on my arm where Fiona's dog had jumped on me the last time I'd gone to her house. Luckily, the burning sensation gave me something to focus on, and there I found the strength to fight the cold and struggle to get out of what could have become a very stinky, snowy grave.

I flailed until I cleared enough room to move my elbows. Once I could bend my arms, I managed to pull myself forward. Maybe it was just an inch, but it was forward. Again and again I jerked forward. My lungs were begging to let go of the stale breath I'd been holding the whole time, but I knew if I opened my mouth, I would die. Faster and more furiously, I jerked myself forward with my arms. I kicked my legs in the hope of finding a windowsill or something else to push against, but I succeeded only in kicking some unsuspecting kid in the face.

And that was what saved my life.

You had to feel bad for the guy. He was probably standing there in pitch blackness, wondering why the emergency lights hadn't come on yet, when out of nowhere this idiot who tried to jump out the window kicks him in the face. So he did what anyone would do in that situation. He hit me back.

In frustration, he grabbed both my feet and shoved them into the snow. That shove, combined with my pulling, allowed me to pop my head out the other side and into fresh air — or as fresh as the air around a two-story pile of rotten-smelling snow can be. Needless to say, at that moment my lungs weren't being picky.

I took long breaths, spraying a mist of brown salty snow with every exhale. I was safe for the moment, though I realized I was hanging about four feet off the ground and everything from my waist down was still firmly encased in the wall of snow.

As I wriggled to free myself, I heard voices to my right . . . or was it my left? I shook my head and cleared two deposits of snow that had wormed their way into my ears. I quickly identified the voices as those of Ultraviolet and Coldsnap. They were standing in the school courtyard somewhere in front of me, though I wasn't sure exactly where. The salt made my eyes burn, and when I tried to wipe them clean, I was only reminded that my hands had been buried in the disgusting snow as well.

"Now, now," Coldsnap reasoned, "there's no need for violence. I just wanted to get your attention so we could talk."

"How about we talk after I take you to jail?"

"Oooh, the cold shoulder. That's my department,

babe." He paused. "Because I'm 'cold.' Get it? You have no sense of humor."

"Whatever you want to say, make it fast."

"Okay, I guess you've figured out I didn't come here for the petty cash I took from that bank. I pay more for one of these suits than I got outta that place. No, I'm going for the big score. The Princess. She's worth millions. But the thing is, I'd appreciate you not screwing it up for me."

"And why would I agree to that?"

"For starters, I'll show you I'm not that bad a guy by letting everyone out of the school." He snapped his fingers and the walls of snow sloughed away from the building. While I imagined that that was a relief for everyone still trapped inside the school, I found it to be a bit like getting caught in a large wave at the beach. I was jostled and tossed, and I rolled across the courtyard for fifteen or twenty feet before I finally came to a rest near Ultraviolet and Coldsnap. If they noticed me, though, they didn't say anything.

"If you're just going to let everyone go, why do it in the first place?" Ultraviolet asked suspiciously.

"I told you, I needed to get your attention. So, do we have a deal?"

"No! I can't just agree to let you commit a robbery."

"I was afraid of that. That's why I have to admit the snow on the school wasn't just to get *your* attention." He gestured to his left, where hundreds of students were climbing out the windows of classrooms and dashing through the exit doors. A news helicopter hovered above the school. Kids were running into the parking lot, where two news stations' vans were arriving. "I had to get their attention, too."

And he snapped his fingers.

The Best Plan? Crash a Helicopter into a School

A buildup of ice on a helicopter's rotors takes only seconds to throw the whole thing's balance into chaos. Coldsnap managed to hit the main rotor with ice crystals that grew exponentially even as huge chunks broke free from the spinning blades and flew off in all directions. Several of those chunks peppered the tail and rear rotor, punching holes in them.

Cap'n Norm and the Sky6 helicopter spun like a bird caught in a tornado, with nowhere to go but down. Down, that was, into the courtyard, where hundreds of students were running to escape the school in which they'd been trapped.

"Better hurry," Coldsnap told Ultraviolet. She flew toward the wounded helicopter in a flash. Meanwhile, Coldsnap casually snapped his fingers, creating a long ice slide that began in the school courtyard and ran off to the east. Coldsnap took a running leap onto it, slipping effortlessly away. As he went, the slide continuously formed in front of him, allowing him to follow it around the side of the school building and wherever he wanted to go from there.

Ultraviolet managed to grab the helicopter, but she nearly tore the skids off the bottom trying to stop it from spinning. Bracing it on her back, she held it steady, but the engine wouldn't shut down. With no other choice available, Ultraviolet punched her fist through the bottom of the cockpit and into the control panel, then yanked wires and circuit boards until the engine cut in a long, drawn-out whine.

Finally, she was able to set the helicopter down gently on the grass. Then she threw open the door and checked Cap'n Norm, who was slumped over the controls, unconscious.

That was when the screams started.

In the parking lot on the opposite side of the courtyard, the news vans found that Coldsnap had left them a surprise. The asphalt was coated with a layer of black ice. No sooner had Ultraviolet released the helicopter than she was streaking across the schoolyard, skimming over the tops of students' heads to get to the parking lot.

With my stinging bloodshot eyes, I could barely make out that she snatched one girl out of the way of the van from Newschannel 9 just before it slid sideways into a parked car, causing a chain reaction of cars sliding along the ice, each bumping the one in the next parking space, setting off a symphony of alarms. After safely dropping the girl, Ultraviolet threw herself into the Eyewitness 13 van, caving in the side doors, but stopping it before it barreled through a crowd of screaming eighth graders.

Taking a moment to readjust her costume, Ultraviolet floated above the wreckage and surveyed the scene. There were two banged-up vans, an entire row of dented cars, a helicopter that would never fly again, hundreds of traumatized students, and an entire schoolyard full of sloppy brown ooze. Once it was apparent that everything was under control and paramedics were arriving, Ultraviolet pounded her fist into her palm and streaked off into the sky in the direction of the Historical Society Museum.

"Nate!" Fiona shouted. "What happened to you?"

"Huh?" It took me a moment to process her

question. I had forgotten that I was shivering in clothes soaked in melted snow, and that my eyes were bright red and my lips were seriously chapped from all the salt.

"Oh, I got away," I said simply.

"Come on," she coaxed, taking my arm. "Let's find Teddy and get you some dry clothes."

We wandered the yard. Some teachers were trying to regain order, calling out to students they recognized and organizing them into little clusters. Fiona pointed out Mr. Reynolds, our math teacher, and we found Teddy nearby.

"Whoa, Nate! What happened?"

"Snow," was all I could manage through my chattering teeth.

"We should probably get him to the school nurse," Fiona suggested. Teddy nodded in agreement.

"Man, looks like Colleen Collins missed out again," Teddy chuckled. "I guess now she knows that if she wants to meet Ultraviolet, the best plan is to try to crash a helicopter into a school full of kids."

I stopped walking. "Oh, no."

"What?" Teddy asked. "Nate, I was just kidding. She's not going to crash into—"

"No," I wheezed. "Colleen Collins."

Fiona and Teddy shrugged at each other. "You're going to have to give us more to go on than that," she prompted.

"Coldsnap's not stupid," I told them. "Why would he tell Ultraviolet where he was going?"

"What are you talking about?" Fiona asked, and I realized she and Teddy hadn't been outside to hear the conversation.

"Coldsnap said he was going to steal the Princess, but if he was really going to steal the Princess diamond, why would he tell her?"

"You think it's a trap?" Teddy asked.

"No, I think the diamond is a distraction. He's going to kidnap the 'American princess,' Colleen Collins."

"How do you figure that?"

"He said, 'She's worth millions.' Not 'it,' 'she.'"

My friends weighed my words for a few moments. "Maybe he meant it the way people call a boat 'she,'" Teddy suggested.

"No, it makes sense," Fiona noted. "The bank robbery and the attack on the school were both attempts to show up Ultraviolet. He wants to embarrass her and prove she can't stop him, so he tells her what he's going to do . . . kind of."

"And then when he gets away with it, he can laugh that much harder," I concluded.

"How can we get word to Ultraviolet?" Teddy said.

Fiona suggested, "We can call the museum and tell them to pass a message—Nate, where are you going?"

With a new focus, I managed to shake off the chills. I marched back into the school, throwing open both doors at once. Teddy and Fiona ran to keep up with me.

"Is there some kind of plan here?" Fiona asked. "Because I'd feel a lot better if I knew what the plan was."

I walked as quickly as I could through the halls, leaving watery brown sneaker marks along the way, until I reached the exit on the opposite side of the building. Parked in the side lot were two school buses. I walked up to one and rapped on the door. The driver looked at me in surprise, then swung the door open.

His scalp was still covered in a patchwork of stitches and his arm had a brace on it, but Mr. Mazzilli was dedicated to his job. He was pouring coffee out of a thermos, which must have held a gallon of the stuff, into the cup that served as its cap. "Hey, kid! What happened to you?"

"Snow," Teddy answered for me as he and Fiona climbed aboard.

"Remember the other night when you said you owed me one?" I asked him.

"Yeah," he replied, dropping his smile and getting serious.

"Well, I need you to drive us over to Ditko. Now."

"I don't know if I can—"

"Somebody's life is in danger."

Our eyes locked and I could tell he was trying to see if I was joking. Finally, he screwed the cap back on his thermos and swung the door shut. "Better hang on tight," he warned.

Coldsnap Tenders His Resignation

The bus pulled into the parking lot of Ditko Middle School and settled in beside a cement mixer. Before Mr. Mazzilli could even open the door all the way, I was forcing my way out. I spotted Colleen Collins almost immediately — there was only one pink hard hat on the construction site — and ran to her.

The foreman gestured to a crane that was lifting a steel girder in place. "We're just not equipped for this kind of cold, Miss Collins. If it gets any worse, I'm going to have to shut down the site."

"Fine," Colleen sighed as if giving in to an unreasonable demand. She stopped to pose for a cameraman from the newspaper. "How much extra am I going to have to pay to keep you working?"

"No, ma'am, you don't understand," the foreman warned. "If that concrete cures at this temperature, next summer, when it hits one hundred ten, the building's foundation is going to crack. Plus the snow is playing havoc with some of the vehicles."

"Very well," Colleen said, relenting. She struck another pose and held it until the photographer snapped a few shots. "Let's just hope the snow lets up soon."

As I ran up to her, I was nearly tackled by one of her huge bodyguards. "Miss Collins! Colleen! It's me! Nate Banks!"

For once, she was the one with the surprised expression. "Nate?" She stared at the sky as if she thought I was there to spring a surprise visit from Ultraviolet on her. "Ewww, what happened to you? You stink and you look awful. Don't you have school today?"

"I don't have time to explain," I urged her. "I need you to get into this bus with me so we can get you somewhere safe."

"What?" she said. "Why would I do that? I have three of my bodyguards with me. There's totally nowhere safer I could be."

I surveyed the site and her limousine but saw only two bodyguards, both the size of buffalo and clearly almost as smart. Then the limousine's passenger-side door opened and the third guard emerged, watching me intently over the blue lenses of his sunglasses.

My heart fell into my stomach. The bodyguard seemed confused at first, then sighed deeply, realizing his secret was out.

"Oh, darn," he muttered sarcastically, snapping his fingers for emphasis. "I guess the plan's going to have to change."

As soon as he snapped his fingers, cold winds whipped around him, encrusting his hair and goatee with snowflakes that formed into long crystals of ice. His skin tone changed from a spray-on tan to a light blue. The only difference from his appearance at the school was that he now wore the black suit of Colleen Collins's bodyguards instead of his trademark custom-tailored silver-and-blue suit.

I tried to shout a warning, but he snapped his fingers and pointed at me. Instantaneously, my mouth was filled with a snowball.

He rushed his employer, alerting the other body-guards. Neither stood a chance against him, though.

Two snaps of his fingers and both of the ox-sized men were encased in inch-thick ice.

"Miss Collins," he hollered. "I'm afraid I have to tender my resignation from your bodyguard detail."

Colleen Collins had been staring up at the crane when she heard him, but when her gaze fell upon the severely altered version of her bodyguard, she stiffened. "What is this? Get away from me!"

Coldsnap blasted the foreman with a pile of snow from his palm, hurling the man's hard hat into a ditch full of wet cement. Another snap of his fingers coated the crane's cables in an icy veneer. Having finally spit all of the snow from my mouth, I shouted warnings to the other construction workers.

While Coldsnap slid along an ice slide to the limousine, with Colleen Collins tossed over his shoulder, the ice spread across and into the cables. With the growth of every crystal of ice, the steel in the cable strained a bit more. Once the first crack formed, there was no stopping the rest. The cable began snapping with a series of pings that sounded like a piano tumbling down a flight of stairs. The girders that had been attached to the cable fell from about four stories up onto two pickup trucks and a portable toilet, splitting all three nearly clean through.

I dove into the pit of wet cement to avoid the girder, adding a layer of thick gray chunks to my already ruined clothes. The cameraman emerged not far from me, his camera destroyed.

The limousine was gone.

I got back to the bus and found that Mr. Mazzilli and my friends had tried to follow Coldsnap, but were stuck spinning their wheels on four patches of ice. Climbing aboard, I wanted to scream, but couldn't find the energy. I collapsed into one of the seats and threw up my hands in disgust. "So close! Why wouldn't she just listen? I'm telling her that her life is in danger and she says I stink!"

"Well, in her defense . . ." Fiona grimaced, gesturing at me.

"Yeah," Teddy agreed. "As long as we're near your house, why don't you grab a change of clothes? I can't take that smell much longer."

"Sorry about that," chuckled Mr. Mazzilli, picking up his lunch box from under his seat. "That's my lunch. The missus made me a Reuben. She pickles her own kraut. It's delicious, but mighty pungent." He opened the lunch box and held out the sandwich wrapped in waxed paper.

"No, it's not your sandwich," Teddy said. "It's that snow. I don't know what's wrong with it, but—"

"Hold on!" Fiona shouted, holding up both hands for quiet. Her eyes darted back and forth like she was calculating something in her head. She reached out and took the sandwich from Mr. Mazzilli's hand, peeled back the waxed paper, and buried her nose in it, sniffing deeply.

Then she stood up and grabbed the bottom of my shirt. She lifted it to her nose and took another deep sniff. She went back and forth a few times, her eyes widening. "This sandwich," she said, shaking it at Mr. Mazzilli. "Corned beef and sauerkraut."

"Yeah, it's a Reuben, like I said."

"That smell in the snow is sauerkraut," Fiona announced triumphantly.

I sat up and sniffed the sandwich myself. "That would explain why it was so salty," I added. Piece by piece, I began to understand. "To use his powers, Coldsnap has to pull moisture from the air around him. But to carry on a snowstorm for a whole city—especially a city in the desert—to do that, he'd need more than just his powers. He'd need a lot of water."

"He'd have to have some kind of hideout set up near the city reservoir," Fiona added, continuing my train of thought. "That's the only place to get enough water for something like this. And that's exactly where the old E&O Binder sauerkraut plant is."

"Right. It's been abandoned for years. It would be the perfect place for a supervillain to hide out and plot his master plan."

"I'm not following you," Teddy interrupted. "Why would that make the snow stink?"

"If he's pulling water out of the reservoir into the plant, it's mixing with the old sauerkraut . . . um . . ."

"Brine," Mr. Mazzilli offered. "The liquid they make sauerkraut in is called brine. It's mostly just salt water until you add the cabbage."

"The snow is a mixture of water and brine. That's why it stinks, and that's why it doesn't freeze completely," Fiona remarked. "It's like Mrs. Sutcliffe was saying about how they put salt on icy roads. The salt in the snow keeps it from forming into anything but mush."

Teddy thought for a second. "I'm still not sure I

understand why he's making stinky snow," he said. "But I think what you're saying is we know where the bad guy's hideout is, right?"

I smiled.

"Does this mean we get to save the day?"

I nodded.

"Can we go get you a change of clothes first?"

You'll Never Get Out That
Sauerkraut Smell

The stream of brown flakes pouring from the roof of the E&O Binder factory told us we were in the right place. Mr. Mazzilli wound the bus around the serpentine roads leading up the hill to the industrial area at the top. "How close do you want me to get?" he asked. "This isn't the most subtle transportation you could have chosen."

The plant had a huge parking lot. Near the front of the building was a giant statue of a traditional sauerkraut crock, which looked a bit like someone had lopped the top off a grain silo. Next to the crock, there were statues of a happy man, woman, and two children, all thrusting forks skyward as if praising their pickled-cabbage deity. "Can you get inside the gates, but keep that statue between us and the main factory?"

Slowly and skillfully, Mr. Mazzilli guided the bus into the lot while keeping us out of sight of anyone who might be in the factory.

"You sure you don't want to try calling the police one more time?" Mr. Mazzilli pleaded.

While I'd been changing into dry clothes, I had called the police.

"Kanigher Falls PD, Detective Hemm," a woman's voice had answered.

"Yes, I'd like to report a kidnapping."

"Uh, okay, were you a witness?"

"Yes, it just happened a few minutes ago."

"And where did this take place?"

"The construction site at Ditko Middle School. Coldsnap kidnapped Colleen Collins and took her to the old sauerkraut factory near the reservoir."

There was a long pause on the other end. "Shouldn't you be in school right now?"

"Look, if you could just send some officers—and get word to Ultraviolet—"

"Listen, kid, I know you probably think this is

funny, but you're committing a felony right now," she growled. "You're interfering with police duties. We're already spread thin today. We have half the station staking out the Princess diamond because we had a threat made against it. Then we have a school on lockdown after an attack and a lot of property damage. Add to that all the fender benders that keep getting called in because no one in this state has snow tires, and the fact that a half dozen officers are out with hypothermia and pneumonia after being attacked by snowmen—and don't even think of laughing. Until you've been buried under a mound of this toxic slush, you have no idea how bad it is."

"Trust me, I know!" I replied.

"And we just got a report of an accident on a construction site, so we're scrambling to find someone to cover that. So, in short, this is not a good day for your little jokes, mister!"

"It's not a joke," I insisted.

"Right. Well, as soon as I get a chance, I'll send Ultraviolet up to the coleslaw factory. Now I'm going to hang up before I'm obligated to come arrest you, because, frankly, I don't have the men to do it."

And the line had gone dead.

"You can try, but I'd rather face Coldsnap than that lady again," I told the driver.

We opened the door and stepped out, making sure to stay behind the statue of the giant sauerkraut crock. "Are you sure you don't want me to come with you?" Mr. Mazzilli called. He sounded concerned for our safety, but also a bit relieved.

"You're the only one who knows how to drive," Fiona said. "Keep the engine on and if you see any of us running out of there screaming in terror, be prepared to floor it."

Mr. Mazzilli nodded, then pulled out his lunch box and coffee thermos to help him pass the time.

We made our way around the back of the plant, skirting along the edge of the city reservoir. Three large concrete pipes connected the factory directly to the huge body of water. Years earlier, E&O Binder would have sucked up thousands of gallons of water a day through those pipes, purified it, and used it to brine cabbage in vats large enough to hold a family of elephants. Now the pumps were humming again, and they were feeding the factory once more. Considering how I had smelled earlier, though, I could tell that someone was obviously skipping the purification process.

"That door's open," Teddy whispered, pointing at a rolling door on the loading dock. It stood about six inches higher than three others like it. Crouching and running at the same time, we got to the door and peeked inside. There was nothing to see but the empty loading area, but inside we could hear the constant mechanical hum of the water pumps and, in the distance, Coldsnap's voice.

We eased the door open a bit more, feeling secure that whatever noise it made would be drowned out by the machinery, and crawled inside. Sticking to the shadows, we made our way to the factory floor.

Coldsnap was decked out in his blue-and-silver suit again. He was standing between two huge vats that looked like they hadn't been cleaned in years, probably because they hadn't been cleaned in years. The pipes were pouring hundreds of gallons of water into them every minute, churning up the filthy brine that remained and had been stagnating and fermenting for years. Coldsnap waved his arms constantly, summoning the snow that zipped up into the air and out a skylight.

"I'm just thinking maybe we've made our point," he said into a cell phone headset that hung on his right ear. "I mean, I made it snow in the desert for a whole day. Let's move on to something else."

I scanned the factory for any hint of where he might be keeping Colleen Collins. "Any ideas?" I asked my friends. They both shook their heads.

"No, if you want more snow, I'll give you more snow. As long as the checks clear, I do what I'm paid to do," Coldsnap told the person on the other end of the line. "It's just that you went to all that trouble augmenting my powers, and I'm using them to make a winter wonderland. A stinky winter wonderland."

Teddy jabbed me in the side and pointed to a staircase that led to an office above us. Through the window, we could see a blond woman sitting in a chair.

"More than anything, I just want to get this job over with so I can take a weeklong shower," Coldsnap laughed. "I'm going to have to burn this suit. No amount of dry cleaning is ever going to get out that sauerkraut smell."

"Teddy, go back to Mr. Mazzilli and tell him to pull around to the front entrance. I'll get Colleen Collins, bring her outside, and meet you at that door." I pointed to an exit near the bottom of the stairs. "Fiona, you stay here and cover me. If anything goes wrong, go back out the way we came in and let Teddy and Mr. Mazzilli know."

They both nodded and Teddy slipped back out the loading dock door.

"You're the boss," Coldsnap went on. "All I'm saying is when Ultraviolet shows up to save the American princess, I've got a surprise for her! Don't worry — I'm not going to ruin the plan. But seriously, which plan is this? Forget about Plan B; we're on, like, Plan N by now."

I hid behind a bunch of old crates as I slipped around the banister and crept up the stairs. Coldsnap was too busy yapping into his cell phone to notice me. When I reached the top landing, I slowly turned the brass doorknob and squeezed into the room, opening the door as little as possible.

"If this doesn't work, I don't know what else we can try," Colleen Collins was saying into her cell phone. "If I have to date another Golden Globe best actor winner, I'm going to scream."

"Ms. Collins," I whispered. She spun around, clearly shocked to find she was no longer alone.

"What? How did you get in here?" Then, into her cell phone, she said, "Um, there's a boy here from the school I'm helping rebuild, Mom. So why don't I let you go?" She pressed the red disconnect button and put her phone back into her pink purse.

"He let you keep your cell phone?" I asked in disbelief. "Why didn't you call 911?"

Colleen's eyes opened wide as if the thought had never occurred to her. "I . . . My mom called and I was talking to her? I guess when we finished maybe I would have thought of that, but she, like, had a problem with her chef? He was making hamburgers with cheese on them and trying to pass them off as cheeseburg—"

"I'm here to help you escape," I said, cutting her off.

"Is Ultraviolet here?" she asked excitedly.

"No, it's just me and my friends. Now follow me downstairs."

"Just you and your friends?" Her excitement turned to irritation.

"Well, there's a bus driver, too," I admitted. "They'll all be waiting outside the door at the bottom of the stairs."

Colleen got a thoughtful look on her face, as if she was debating whether she wanted to be rescued or not. "See, here's the thing," she explained. "I'd feel better about this if Ultraviolet was here. Why didn't you go get her to save me?"

"I tried, but she's protecting the Princess diamond, because the entire police force is convinced Coldsnap is going to try to steal it. I tried to call the police but—" Suddenly, I had an idea. If I couldn't convince the police that Colleen Collins had been kidnapped, maybe a call from her own cell phone would. I grabbed her purse and pulled out the phone, narrowly avoiding the nipping jaws of her dog.

"What are you doing?" she demanded.

"Calling the police. If we can convince them you've really been kidnapped, they'll send everyone, and that includes Ultraviolet." I accidentally hit the green send button before I dialed, bringing up the number of the last incoming call, from Colleen's mom. The phone connected and I was about to press the red button to hang up when I heard a ringing behind me.

Right outside the door to the office, a big band tune

played. The door swung open and Coldsnap stepped inside. He held up his phone to see who the call was from and grinned wickedly before rejecting it.

"Kid, when are you going to learn to just give up?"

I imagined Doctor Nocturne was going to ask me the same thing if I ever survived to see him again.

Brain Freeze

I was finally putting the pieces together, but it was too late for it to matter. Colleen Collins and Coldsnap had been working together the entire time.

"Where's Ultraviolet, kid?" Coldsnap prodded.

"I told you. She's at the museum protecting the Princess diamond. You told her yourself you were going to steal it."

"Why would you tell her that?" Colleen asked him angrily.

"I was buying myself some time," he explained. "If I told her I was going directly after you, she would have caught me before I even got there. But I figured they'd realize I wasn't at the museum soon enough."

"That's why she didn't show up to stop you at the construction site," Colleen growled. *"We're going to have to improv,"* she said, deepening her voice to sound like a slower, stupider version of Coldsnap's. *"I don't know why she's not here, but we're going to have to go through with the kidnapping anyway."*

"It's not my fault," he argued. "She should have figured out the diamond was a red herring once you got kidnapped."

"No one even knows she's been kidnapped," I said. "You've caused so much chaos in this town, no one noticed when you kidnapped her. When I tried to report it, the police accused me of lying and said they'd arrest *me!*"

"So now what are we going to do?" Coldsnap asked. "If Ultraviolet doesn't show up, the plan's out the window."

"Let me think," Colleen snarled. She tapped her lower lip while she paced for about thirty seconds. "Okay, I've got a new plan."

Coldsnap pushed my back, urging me down the stairs. I glanced toward the loading docks and didn't see Fiona, which made me hopeful she was getting help. Colleen Collins began to lay out a plot in which Coldsnap would head to the museum, then lure Ultraviolet back to the factory. As she spoke, though, I heard a noise that was out of place. Over the sound of the machinery, I could make out a high-pitched whistle that sounded like a bomb falling from the sky.

"You know," I interrupted, "I don't think you're going to have to worry about that backup plan."

The skylight shattered, raining glass down into the vats. My first thought was that a meteor had hit the factory, as the floor trembled and cracked with the impact. But instead of a chunk of space rock in the center of the spiderweb cracks in the concrete floor, there was Ultraviolet.

"Coldsnap," she said through a forced grin. "Did that get your attention?"

Ultraviolet grabbed the base of one of the brine vaults and tore it from its foundation. Instinctively, I found cover. She hurled the metal cauldron at Coldsnap, spilling stagnant brine all over the floor. With a snap of his fingers, he raised a wall of ice that grew around the vat, holding it in midair. Another vat of brine came at him and was deflected, tearing through the wall of the factory.

"Oh, goodness," Colleen shouted, pretending to be innocent. "Thank heavens Ultraviolet is here to save me!"

Ultraviolet paid no attention to Colleen. Instead, she charged Coldsnap at supersonic speed. He blasted her with a casing of ice, but this time she was prepared, shaking it off in midflight and still managing to tackle him about the waist, knocking him through the hole in the wall and into the parking lot. I ran out after them.

Coldsnap stood up slowly. "That hurt," he told Ultraviolet. "I think I twisted my ankle."

"You can put some ice on it later," she deadpanned.

"Maybe you do have a sense of humor," Coldsnap said. "It's not a very good one, but it's still a nice try."

Ultraviolet drew back her fist and lunged at him.

He snapped fingers on both hands just as Ultraviolet got close. Snow from all around swarmed Ultraviolet, trapping her. The more snow that joined the mass, the harder it became to see her. Within seconds, all anyone could see was a heaving, swirling tunnel of snow that doubled back on itself. Coldsnap admired his work with smug enthusiasm.

"All right," he said. "I was saving this for a special occasion, and I guess this is it."

"What is 'this'?" Colleen asked, running to join us as quickly as her pink high heels would let her.

"Have you ever been in an avalanche?" Coldsnap posed the question to us both. "That's a rhetorical question. If either of you had, you'd probably be dead, so let me explain. When you're caught in an avalanche, the snow becomes like water. It's impossible to fight the current, because there's nothing to brace yourself against. This is an avalanche in a convenient, portable form."

Colleen stepped forward to examine the spinning snow.

"I wouldn't get too close," warned Coldsnap. "Ultraviolet is trying to fly out of there, but the faster she flies, the faster the snow moves. Think of it like a treadmill. No matter how fast or how slow she goes, the snow will match her speed and keep her suspended forever. Or until she dies. I'm not sure how long she can hold her breath."

"Wait, that's not the plan," Colleen protested.

"Plans change. You want me to just let her punch me in the face and drag me to jail? I gave her a fighting chance, and she lost."

"Let her go!" I shouted, rushing Coldsnap and knocking him to the ground.

He yelped, probably because he twisted the same

ankle again. "You know, kid, I told you when to quit and you didn't." He extended his fingers, pantomiming a gun, and held them to my head. He snapped his fingers on the opposite hand.

My brain felt like it was turning inside out. I flopped onto the ground, clutching both temples and scrunching my eyes closed as tightly as possible. The pain was unbearable.

"And you thought brain freeze from a milkshake was bad," Coldsnap laughed.

I pounded my head against the asphalt. It didn't feel good, but it felt different, which was an improvement. I struggled to my knees, but my balance was too far gone to risk getting to my feet. My stomach flip-flopped and I thought I would throw up. Then I thought that might not be so bad, since at least the vomit would be warm.

"The whole point of this was for Ultraviolet to save me," Colleen shouted. "If you kill her, how am I going to get on the cover of *Famous Faces* with her?"

"Sorry, but I'm looking at the big picture, boss. Superheroes are bad for my business, and if I have the chance to get rid of one, I can't give that up for a photo op."

I looked at Ultraviolet's snow cocoon through squinted eyes. I couldn't quite make it out. It was just a white blur with a large yellow-and-black blur behind it. And that blur seemed to be getting larger.

An air horn blared and brakes squealed as the bus smashed into the portable avalanche and Ultraviolet, destroying its own front end. If hitting Ultraviolet at forty miles per hour wasn't enough to smash the grille, add the power of an avalanche smashing down on the hood at over one hundred miles per hour. The crash sent Ultraviolet flying across the parking lot, where she skidded to a stop near me. She was perfectly still. I tried to see if she was breathing, but the coldness in the core of my brain kept me from concentrating on anything for more than a few seconds at a time.

The avalanche picked apart the bus, tearing out every nut, bolt, gear, and belt from the tires forward. Teddy, Fiona, and Mr. Mazzilli leapt out the rear emergency exit to safety, or at least as much safety as anyone can find in a parking lot with a snow tunnel spewing bus parts into the air at the speed of a major league fastball.

Through my squinted eyes, I could see Teddy

walking defiantly up to Coldsnap. In his hands, he carried Mr. Mazzilli's thermos. "Oh, what a great friend you must be," Coldsnap said, taunting him. "Hide on the bus the whole time and let your buddy get taken hostage and beaten up."

"No," Teddy informed him, "I'm a great friend because when my buddy needs me, I save the day." With that, he hurled the steaming contents of the thermos into Coldsnap's face. If Teddy had expected the coffee to burn Coldsnap, he would have been disappointed. By the time it got within an inch of the villain's face, it vaporized, leaving nothing but a cloud around Coldsnap's head that fogged up his glasses.

"Ooooh, I'm melting!" Coldsnap joked, reaching up to wipe the haze from his glasses.

When he did, Teddy swung the gallon-sized metal thermos with both arms, smashing it against Coldsnap's head. The supervillain dropped to his knees.

Coldsnap shook his head a few times and rubbed the side of it. He got back up, angrily pointing one hand at Teddy and extending the other back to snap his fingers. "I was going to let you live, kid—"

The next thing I heard, though, wasn't a snap; it was the sound of crunching finger bones. A panting and worn but very much alive Ultraviolet had grabbed Coldsnap's hand and spun him around to face her. She drew back her arm and landed one punch squarely in Coldsnap's face, laying him out.

That's Prepostosaurus!

We could hear sirens from the bottom of the hill. A snake of police cars, ambulances, fire trucks, and slightly damaged news vans wound its way up the road toward us. Colleen Collins quickly checked her hair and makeup in a compact. "Ultraviolet! It's so good to finally meet you," she oozed sweetly. "I can't wait to tell everyone how you saved me."

"That really won't be necessary," Ultraviolet insisted.

"Oh, it's no problem at all." She examined the superheroine and offered her some lip gloss. "You have a little something in your hair," she said, reaching up to pluck something from Ultraviolet's head. Ultraviolet pushed her away, but Colleen Collins seemed unconcerned, like she was used to people being annoyed with her. She dropped her hand into her purse as though she was saving Ultraviolet's hair gunk as a souvenir.

"Now, when the press gets here, let me go first. I'll tell them how scared I was and how Ultraviolet herself realized how much danger I was in—"

"Are you going to tell them you planned the whole thing?" I asked. "Or should I?"

Colleen froze. "What did you say?"

"Are you planning to tell them you hired Coldsnap to kidnap you just so you could meet Ultraviolet?"

"Nate, that's prepost—prepostosaurus—that's stupid. Why would you say something like that?"

"This was all about getting on the cover of the celebrity magazines," I explained to Ultraviolet and my friends. "Her popularity has been slipping ever since her album bombed."

"It was huge in Europe . . . and Azerbaijan!" she insisted.

"Ultraviolet is the newest superhero, who avoids all publicity. So Colleen Collins decided the best way to get herself back in the public eye would be to meet up with Ultraviolet and get the story in the media. But when Ultraviolet refused an invitation to the groundbreaking ceremony, she concocted a new plan. She hired Coldsnap to be one of her bodyguards so he could 'kidnap' her. Then Ultraviolet would have no choice but to show up to rescue her."

The sirens drew closer.

I continued. "I'll bet they were about to spring the plan into action after the groundbreaking when she saw me and thought of yet another option. If she buttered me up enough, maybe I would talk Ultraviolet into coming to a party or having lunch or doing something else that would give her the chance to snap a bunch of photos together and try to convince the world that she was worth paying attention to for one more week. But I didn't work fast enough."

Colleen's face was as red as the approaching fire trucks.

"That's why she invited us to the diamond installation at the history museum. She was monitoring me. And when she became convinced I wouldn't be able to bring her to Ultraviolet, she decided to bring Ultraviolet to her. Coldsnap coated the Moldoff Bridge with a thin layer of ice right in front of our bus because she expected Ultraviolet to rescue us. That's why she was on the scene, hoping one of her publicists could get a shot of her and Ultraviolet pulling kids to safety together."

"Except Ultraviolet never showed up at the bus crash," Colleen argued, pointing an accusing finger at the superheroine.

"Which is why you went back to your original plan," I answered. "You unleashed Coldsnap on the city with the intention of getting Ultraviolet's attention and making things personal. You told him to rob the bank where I was with my dad, and you told him to attack our school, because you thought Ultraviolet would be more likely to respond if I was in danger. Then he was supposed to kidnap you right in front of that photographer from the newspaper, but you were counting on the fact that Ultraviolet would be so upset by Coldsnap getting away twice that she wouldn't risk letting him pull off another crime."

"If only that were true," she said innocently.

"Except by that point, your plans had become so knotted, and Coldsnap had created so much chaos, that Ultraviolet was busy trying to protect your diamond instead of saving you, leaving you to scramble for yet another plan."

Colleen's face turned defiant. "That's all speculation. You have no proof. If you say any of that to these reporters, my lawyers will bury you. You won't see anything but the inside of a courtroom until you're sixty."

I had a sudden realization. "Hey." I turned to Ultraviolet. "How did you figure out Coldsnap wasn't going for the diamond after all?"

"After about an hour, one of the police officers noticed the Princess diamond was melting. We realized Coldsnap had already—"

"Melting?" Colleen Collins interrupted, a vein throbbing in her temple. "What do you mean, 'melting'? Diamonds are the hardest substance on Earth. For a diamond to melt, it would pretty much have to be on the sun."

"Yes," Ultraviolet agreed, "but a cleverly crafted decoy of the diamond made out of ice will melt at room temperature."

Colleen Collins spun and scowled at the limp form of Coldsnap, but with the news crews arriving, she couldn't be found throttling an unconscious man and screaming at him for being a double-crosser. While she was distracted, Ultraviolet gave Teddy, Fiona, and me a silent wave and flew into the clouds.

The camera crews hustled from their vans, and Colleen's broad phony smile returned. "Let me just say how thankful I am to Ultraviolet, who rescued me and . . . Oh, where is she now? I swear she was just here a minute ago. I guess she had to fly off to save the day somewhere else. She really was here. I mean it. Also, I owe a debt of gratitude to Nate Banks—"

"Actually, I didn't really do much," I interrupted. I turned to face the reporters. "I was just along for the ride. The real hero here today"—I grabbed Teddy's arm and dragged him in front of me—"is Teddy Cochrane."

At once, all the reporters began shooting questions at Teddy, allowing me to fade into the background.

"Why did you do that?" Fiona asked.

"Well, for starters, that thing with the thermos was pretty cool."

"Yeah, but they wanted to talk to you. You were the one who figured out that Colleen was in on it. Why not take some credit?"

"In the last week, I've been in a bus crash, a bank

robbery, and a blizzard all because someone saw me on the news and thought I was close to Ultraviolet. I think maybe I should take a little break from the spotlight for a while." I looked back at Teddy describing Coldsnap's avalanche, spinning his hands around each other manically. "Besides, I promised Teddy something, and I think this should do it."

Fiona thought for a moment, then gasped in disgust. "Allison Heaton's Halloween party?"

"How can she not invite him now?" I said with a laugh.

An angry Colleen Collins stepped between us. "I'm glad you find this all so amusing," she growled. "But there's one thing you should know, little boy." She leaned into my face and spoke without unclenching her jaw. "You think you put together all the pieces, but this is a *big* puzzle, and there are pieces you haven't even seen yet."

She straightened up, pivoted, and marched away, kicking the ribs of the out-cold Coldsnap as she left the scene.

Stay Cool, Kids

We all had to go back to the police station to answer some questions and fill out some paperwork. Teddy, Fiona, and I sat at a table in a room with a mirror on one wall.

"Hey," I said, realizing something. "I never asked how you got Ultraviolet and the cops up to the sauerkraut plant."

"Remember at the school when I suggested we call the museum and ask them to pass along a message to Ultraviolet?" Fiona said.

"Yeah."

"Mr. Mazzilli called the museum and asked them to pass along a message," Teddy said.

I nodded. "Hmm. We'll have to remember that the next time."

Finally, the door opened and a woman in a rumpled suit entered. "Hey, kids. I'm Detective Hemm. I appreciate you being so patient while we get everything straightened out." She shook each of our hands weakly. "You already filled out these statements, and it looks like any truancy charges are going to be dropped—"

"Truancy?" Fiona challenged, but she was dismissed with a wave of the detective's hand.

"I told you, the charges are being dropped, in light of the assistance you provided while you were absent from school without permission."

She glared at the mirror, and after a moment I realized that it wasn't the mirror but someone behind it who was getting the stink eye.

"Officially, I'm in here to offer a formal apology on behalf of the Kanigher Falls Police Department in addition to a personal apology for my conduct on the phone earlier."

I sat up in my chair, suddenly recognizing her voice.

"It was out of line for me to accuse you of making crank calls or falsely reporting a kidnapping. I hope my actions in no way contributed to your decision to fight a supervillain on your own."

"You're the one?" Fiona barked. "If it weren't for you, we never would have had to go up—"

I put my hand on Fiona's arm to stop her. "It's okay, Detective. It was a bad day for everyone. Just do me a favor?"

"What's that?"

"Promise me that next time I ask you for help, no matter how crazy it sounds, you'll believe whatever I say."

"And why would I want to promise you that?"

"Because if the last month or so has been any indication, I get the feeling we're going to cross paths again."

Detective Hemm escorted us down the hallway and past the holding cells. As we approached, we could see a layer of ice extending out from one of them. Passing by, we saw Coldsnap casually lounging on the bunk inside, though the room looked more like an ice cave than a jail cell. Icicles hung from the ceiling; a sheen of ice covered the cinder block walls; and a light snow filled the air.

When we walked past, it felt like someone had left the door to the freezer open.

"Stay cool, kids," Coldsnap shouted after us. His laughter followed us all the way to the lobby, where our parents were waiting.

While Teddy told his dad about hitting Coldsnap with the thermos and Fiona bragged to her mother about figuring out the sauerkraut connection, I accepted my pat on the back from my parents. But the moment was broken by a man in a dark suit with an aluminum briefcase. He confidently strode in from the parking lot and flashed a badge and government ID to the sergeant behind the desk.

"Agent Steve Jennings," he said, introducing himself. "I'm from the Superhuman Detention Division, and I'm here to pick up Coldsnap."

The sergeant leaned forward to examine the badge. "Oh, right. I haven't seen you guys since we had that Malcontent guy in here. Head on back." He reached beneath the desk, disengaging the lock, and a buzzing noise came from the door to the left.

"Has he given you any trouble?" Agent Jennings asked as he passed through the door.

"Well, we're going to need a mop once that cell

thaws out," the sergeant noted. "But otherwise he's been on his best behavior. Says it's not worth trying to break out, because his boss's lawyers will have him free in twenty-four hours."

I swallowed hard at the thought of Coldsnap's boss and couldn't help wondering just how many more puzzle pieces Colleen Collins had warned me about.

I Dare You

"Teddy!" Allison Heaton cheered as she opened the door. "Everybody, Teddy's here!" Allison, who was dressed as a pirate queen, stood aside to let us in. Fiona, who was also dressed as a pirate queen, sighed as we walked through the door.

Allison looked Teddy and me up and down, apparently not sure what to make of our costumes. "Wow, guys . . . um, what are you supposed to be?"

"We're Hammer and Sickle," Teddy told her as though it was obvious. "But we're in the blue uniforms they wore from 1993 to 1995, when they were Hammer and Sickle Xtreme Team."

"Oh," she said, pretending to care. "Those were good comics?"

"No," Teddy laughed. "They were awful. That's what makes it funny."

Allison fake-laughed politely. "Why don't I introduce you to everybody?" she said, changing the subject and dragging Teddy away by the hand.

"She's holding my hand," he mouthed as he disappeared around the corner into the kitchen.

Most of the people at the party were seventh graders we recognized, even if we didn't know their names. A few Eisner kids were there, too, including some eighth graders who seemed to think they were too cool to be at a Ditko seventh grader's Halloween party, yet they had come anyway.

Fiona and I talked and ate snacks, but for the most part we counted the minutes until we could leave without seeming rude. Someone suggested playing truth or dare, and even though we stood on the fringe of the group, talking to each other, we somehow got roped in.

"Sixth-grade girl," one of the eighth-grade boys from Eisner said, challenging Fiona, "I dare you and your friends to go down the block to Fawcett Lawns, go inside the gate, and stay there for half an hour."

The crowd oohed and aahed. The nicer ones got worried expressions on their faces while the mean ones leaned forward in anticipation of Fiona's breaking down in tears.

Instead, she shot a glance at Teddy and me that said, "Are they kidding?"

"Don't wait up," she answered, standing and heading for the door. I got up as well, and gave Teddy a little nudge.

"Um, I guess I'll be back in half an hour," he said to Allison. He smiled vacantly as he walked backward toward the door so he wouldn't have to take his eyes off hers. Since he wasn't looking where he was going, he ran directly into Meathead, knocking the bully into the food table, where his hand landed in a bowl of onion dip.

"Whoa, sorry about that—" Teddy grimaced as Meathead rose to his full height.

Then a smile broke out across Meathead's face. "Don't sweat it, Teddy. Hey, word on the street is you might know how to get an Ultraviolet autograph."

"Come on, Teddy," Fiona shouted. Teddy scrambled to the door and Meathead waved genially.

"And bring back some proof you were there," an

eighth grader called after us. "You can't just go hide in Mr. Russell's front yard for thirty minutes."

"That party stinks," Fiona complained as we walked to the cemetery.

"No way!" Teddy responded. "That's the best party I've ever been to."

"Teddy, imagine if Allison wasn't there and wasn't flirting with you the whole time," I suggested.

He thought for a few seconds. "Well, that would stink."

Outside the gate to the cemetery, a group of trick-or-treaters was warning one another about the dangers of going inside Fawcett Memorial Lawns. "I heard three kids went in there last week and a zombie caught them and took them all back to his tomb."

"I heard ghosts hid their bikes in the trees so they couldn't get away."

Fiona bulldozed her way through the gathering. "I heard there's some great barbecue in there if you know where to look," she laughed as she pushed open the iron gates.

"Hey, don't go in there!" one of the kids warned. "You'll never come back out!"

Fiona contemplated for a second, then shrugged. "I'll

take my chances." She ducked inside the graveyard to the horror of the younger kids.

Teddy and I shrugged as well, then followed her lead. We walked along the pond, climbed the hill, and knocked on the Zuembay door. The door slowly opened to reveal Captain Zombie dressed as George Washington. He was wearing a full Continental Army uniform that looked authentic—and by that I mean it looked like it was almost 250 years old. He stepped out of the tomb holding a bowl of candy. "Oh, trick-or-treaters, it's about time," he said kindly. "I've been waiting all night for—oh, what's up, guys? I thought you were trick-or-treating. Are you trick-or-treating? Because I have lots of candy, and no one seems to be coming by."

"No," Fiona told him, "we're not trick-or-treating—"

"I'll take some candy, though," Teddy chimed in, and we both grabbed some Milky Ways and little boxes of Nerds.

"We were at a lame party and someone dared me to come to the graveyard," Fiona continued. "So, you want some company?"

Captain Zombie smiled widely, or as widely as the

dried, leathery skin on his face would let him. "Sure! Let's order some pizza."

He stepped aside to let us in. "Oh, and I need to bring back some kind of proof that I was actually here and not just hiding down the street," Fiona said, remembering, as she walked down the stairs.

Captain Zombie thought for a second, then snapped off his right pinkie finger and offered it to her. "Here," he said generously. "I can get a new one."

I tore open a Milky Way and took a bite. Maybe someday my life would go back to normal.

But tonight I was going to eat deep-dish pizza with my best friends and a zombie.

Check out all the action in
Nate's next adventure!

THE AMAZING ADVENTURES OF NATE BANKS
#3: RED ALERT

"I really don't think Stephanie wanted us—"

"Does the term 'secret identity' mean nothing to you?" he barked. Then he turned and continued to climb the ladder up the side of the warehouse. I followed him hesitantly. He wore his full uniform—a blue business suit with a matching cape and fedora—but all I had was a small mask that went around my eyes. I'd added a baseball cap and a hooded sweatshirt, but there was no way I was going to fool anyone into thinking I was a superhero.

"Sorry," I said. "I don't think . . . the *other* Doctor Nocturne would want us doing this."

He stopped climbing and I nearly crashed into him. "Did I give you the impression that I needed my daughter's *permission* to fight crime in my hometown?" he asked gruffly. "I have been this city's symbol of justice for almost sixty years, and no one is going to tell me that I can't stop a simple smuggling operation."

He continued up the ladder and heaved himself over the edge of the roof. I stuck close to him, careful to avoid the skylight so our silhouettes wouldn't alert anyone who might be watching from inside. As he walked, I could tell he was doing his best not to hobble on his bad hip, but with each step, the hitch seemed more noticeable.

When he reached the opposite end of the roof, he crouched behind an air conditioner and peered out toward the docks, where a ship was unloading. As I took my place beside him, he grabbed the back of my shirt and pulled me closer.

"See that big guy on the gangplank?"

I looked at the boat, but couldn't tell what he meant.

"What's a gangplank?" I whispered.

"What's a — it's a gangplank!" he managed to yell without raising his voice above a whisper. He pointed at the ramp from the dock to the boat.

"Oh, that bridge thing."

"Yes, now do you see that big guy who just got to the bottom of 'that bridge thing'?"

Now that I knew where to look, the big guy in question was kind of hard to miss. He stood nearly a head taller than all the sailors, none of whom seemed like small men. He accentuated his height by wearing a top hat and a black suit that drew attention to his long, rail-thin body.

"That's the Mortician," I said, trying to reinforce the idea that I'd been studying the files he gave me. "Eastern European crime lord. Deals largely in fine artwork and . . . um . . . counterfeit money. Earned his name after several competing crime bosses were found in caskets. The caskets also started rumors that he was . . ."

And at that moment, something dawned on me.

I turned to look at the man crouched beside me. They called him Doctor Nocturne because he never was seen in the sunlight. He was old enough to be my great-grandfather, but didn't look much older than my dad. He blended into shadows and moved with barely a sound. He had the ability to cloud people's minds. And he wore a cape! It all fit together perfectly.

I didn't know why I hadn't figured it out sooner. Maybe because he'd been clouding my mind?

"Doctor Nocturne," I said, swallowing hard before continuing. "I have a question."

"What is it now?" he growled, keeping his eyes trained on the Mortician.

"Are you—" I faltered. "Are you a vampire?"

He sighed deeply and cast his eyes upward.

I began to worry how he would react now that I'd discovered his secret. Was I the only one who knew? Had he confided in anyone else other than his daughter?

"I want you to know I'm not afraid," I lied. "I just want to know—"

Suddenly he spun and snarled in my face, "Boy, have you lost your fool mind?! Do I *look* like a vampire to you?"

I didn't dare tell him that when he pulled his lips back to reveal his teeth the way he was just now, they did have a kind of vampiric look to them.

"There's no such thing as a vampire!" he insisted. "You've been reading too many teen romance novels."

"But the Mortician—"

"The Mortician is a pale, creepy-looking guy who goes out of his way to be pale and creepy-looking because he realized it's good for business if his competition is afraid of him. That's it." He turned his attention back to the boat and his frown managed to sink even deeper into his face. "Where did he go?"

I looked, too, but the Mortician was nowhere to be

seen. For that matter, almost everyone was gone except a few sailors who lay on the ground, unconscious.

The siren of a police car wailed in the distance. Doctor Nocturne leapt up, wincing and holding his hip for a split second before he could remind himself not to. If he was in any pain, you would never have guessed it from the way he dashed to the corner of the roof.

Just before he prepared to leap for a fire escape on the next building, a voice called to him from behind us. "Dad! Where are you going?"

He stopped and pivoted in a blur, instinctively raising his fists. When he saw that it was his daughter, wearing a matching blue suit, cape, and fedora, he only lowered them slightly.

"What are you guys doing up here?" she asked. "I thought you were training in the cave."

"My sources told me the Mortician was bringing in a shipment—"

"Yeah, I know," Stephanie replied. "You and I have the same sources, remember?"

The police had arrived below us and were leading a dazed Mortician to their squad car. The older Doctor Nocturne bit his lower lip as he watched.

"I can't believe you brought Nate out here."

"Hey," I protested. "Secret identities."

"Fine, what do you want me to call you? Nocturnal Boy? Kid Nighttime?" she asked, punching each name with a sarcastic tone.

"I guess Nate's okay," I conceded.

"And, Dad, where is your cane?" she prodded, turning her attention back to him.

"I'm fine without that thing."

"No, you're really not," she sighed. "And if you try to jump from one building to another on a bad hip, you'll be lucky if a cane is all you need."

Her father reluctantly backed down. "Come on, boy. Let's head to the cave." He started toward the ladder, and I followed, but Stephanie grabbed me by the shoulder.

"Nate, I know he's supposed to be taking care of you, but you're going to have to keep an eye on him, too. Keep him out of trouble, okay?"

I nodded agreement.

"And make sure he uses his cane."

I felt the lump just above my ear where Doctor Nocturne had rapped me with the cane the day before. "Oh, don't worry," I told her. "He's definitely using it."